Edward Storrow

Our Indian sisters

Edward Storrow

Our Indian sisters

ISBN/EAN: 9783337305222

Printed in Europe, USA, Canada, Australia, Japan

Cover: Foto ©Andreas Hilbeck / pixelio.de

More available books at **www.hansebooks.com**

OUR INDIAN SISTERS

BY THE

REV. E. STORROW

FORMERLY OF THE CALCUTTA MISSION OF THE LONDON MISSIONARY SOCIETY

WITH THIRTY ILLUSTRATIONS

LONDON

THE RELIGIOUS TRACT SOCIETY

56 PATERNOSTER ROW, AND 65 ST. PAUL'S CHURCHYARD

HINDU GIRLS IN AN ORPHANAGE (SOUTH INDIA).

PREFACE

THE genesis of this book may briefly be explained. From the time I became a missionary in Calcutta, in 1848, a series of incidents led me to become deeply interested in the condition of Hindu women. For almost three years I resided with Dr. and Mrs. Mullens. He was an ardent missionary, a zealous worker, and possessed of a rare amount of missionary information. Mrs. Mullens was like-minded; almost all her time was given to her native boarding-school, the visitation of native Christian women, and Hindus, so far as then was practicable.

I was also so fortunate as to become acquainted, at an early date, with Gyanendro Mohun Tagore, a member of a leading family in Calcutta, whose young wife had recently died, avowing her faith in Christ. Her brief history was remarkable and touching, as an illustration of the manner in which Divine truth could find its way into zenanas, and I wrote a memoir of Bala Shoondari Tagore, and of her cousin, who by similar steps was led to the Saviour. Her history was said to have ' profoundly interested many people,' for it was the first known instance of a Hindu lady of rank avowing her faith in Christ, and indicated clearly the manner in which, most probably, Christian truth would find its way into Hindu and Mahomedan families of position.

Her conversion and death led her husband to avow himself a Christian, and gave to my own mind a permanent conviction of the need and importance of Christian effort in behalf of women. I had become interested in Hindu history, mythology, opinion, and life, and this incident, with what I soon saw every-where, drew my attention to the unique position of women, and the hard conditions of their lot. My principal duties as a missionary encouraged sympathy and inquiry in this direction, for during the eighteen years I remained in Calcutta I was more or less engaged in the education of young men, chiefly

belonging to families aspiring to zenana respectability.
To be almost daily in the midst of six hundred youths,
intellectually most receptive, eager for a good education, and sure to have their opinions greatly altered
by it, was to me a position most satisfying and
suggestive ; for I learned through them, indirectly,
much relative to the position of native ladies, and
soon inferred that the most efficient agency for reaching them was to educate on a Christian basis their
sons and brothers.

During the first twenty years of this latter half
of the century female emancipation has most rapidly
advanced, and I had the happiness of being acquainted
more or less with some of the most active leaders of
the movement.

I left India with infinite regret, and with an undying
interest in the people and their evangelization. I
have always been ready to speak and write on these
subjects, and not least on the status of women and
their elevation. I have not been content with the
knowledge I gained whilst in India, but ever since
have read all that was within my reach on these
questions, studied them, and noted whatever seemed
to be of value.

I formed the purpose to write this book some years
ago, when I saw that many English women were interested in the subject, but knew so little about it,
or, indeed, could know, for the sources of information,
though useful as far as they went, were usually
elementary and superficial.

But my task has been most arduous. I wished to
make the book a thorough record of the usages and
ideas governing the condition of women, to give
some explanation of their origin and extent, and to
be as accurate and impartial as possible.

I have been the more careful, knowing how much
there is in all Hindu affairs that is difficult to understand, seemingly contradictory, often contrary to the
intelligence, humanity, and gentleness of the people
themselves, and that educated native gentlemen
usually take a more favourable view of the condition
of native women than we do.

That is the reason why this book so abounds with
quotations from native authorities, ancient and
modern, and is so largely a statement of facts ; for
I have felt it important to fortify whatever is advanced, by opinion less likely to be questioned than
an Englishman's and a missionary's, though I know
of none so accurate and less given to exaggeration.

Another difficulty I have had arises from the fact
that whilst opinion on women throughout all India is
degrading and contemptuous, the usages governing
their condition vary. Among some of the nationalities they are less jealously guarded, have more
personal freedom and a wider family influence, than
in others. The differences, for instance, in the status
and treatment of women in Rajput, Mahratta, Punjabi,
Bengali, Telugu, Tamil, and other great nationalities
are considerable, and suggestive of wide race dis-
tinctions of character and temperament ; but though

interesting, they need not now be pointed out. I have written this book profoundly conscious of the stupendous and pathetic importance of its subject, and pained by the apathy and indifference with which it is regarded. That must be because Europeans know not the facts of the case, or are too selfish to try to realize them.

I am greatly indebted to the Church Missionary Society, the London Missionary Society, and the Zenana Bible and Medical Mission both for supplying electros of engravings and also in some cases placing photographs at my disposal for the illustrations which add so greatly to the value of the book.

If this book should awaken in any a more intelligent and ardent interest in the women of India, and, indeed, in missions generally—for this has been my aim and prayer—I shall feel most grateful to God.

E. STORROW.

NORMAL TRAINING CLASS (NAGERCOIL, SOUTH INDIA).

CONTENTS

LIST OF ILLUSTRATIONS

14   LIST OF ILLUSTRATIONS

INDIAN WOMEN POUNDING RICE.

OUR INDIAN SISTERS

—ⵯ—

CHAPTER I

WOMEN IN THE CODE OF MANU.

IT is necessary to give some account of the origin, age, and authority of this remarkable book, since it embodies the sentiments commonly entertained of women in ancient times, and is chiefly responsible for the subordinate and unhappy position they have held in all subsequent ages.

Manu himself, like so many who appear in ancient Hindu literature, is little more than a name. He may have been the compiler of the Code : he was probably the author of some parts of it, and its permeating genius ; but certainly no one wrote the whole. Portions of it are evidently of various ages, and written by various persons, but who they were, and who (whether one person or a group) finally arranged the whole,

B

and claimed for it divine authority, is one of the insoluble mysteries of Oriental literature.

It is thought by those most capable of forming an opinion that the Code is a collection of laws, rules, and opinions gathered from various sources ; that its original form was not that of a Code, in the modern sense of the word ; that it was compiled by Brahmins with the design of glorifying their order and perpetuating their power ; that it expresses sentiments and opinions on a great variety of domestic, social, sumptuary, and religious questions, with the view of presenting an ideal of what Aryan society should be, from the Brahminical point of view, and in behalf of Brahminical domination ; and that to give it authority and permanence a divine and inspired quality was ascribed to it, as also the form of a Code.[1]

Many portions of the Code are more than 2000 years old, and in its present form it has existed for 1400 years ; nevertheless, the sentiments it expresses relative to women are to-day prevalent, more or less, all over India. It crystallized the suspicion and contempt with which women were regarded in ancient times, and has handed them down in this fixed and evil form to all succeeding ages. Hence the significance and importance attached to it. Through its high claims, its unique form and purpose, the extraordinary astuteness,

---

[1] 'The moral and political code propounded by Manu is reputed to have been revealed to that inspired sage by Brahma himself.'— *Modern India*, by Sir Monier M. Williams, p. 228.

pertinacity, and self-assertion of the most remarkable
sacerdotal caste the world has ever seen, and certain
marked characteristics of the Aryan mind making it
a most receptive soil for such seed, it has impressed
itself on the thoughts and habits of the people as
no other book has, although they have ever been disposed to attach divine or quasi-divine qualities to all
ancient religious books.[1]

Whatever, indeed, may have been its origin, the fact
remains that for more than 1400 years it has held a
place second only to the Vedas, in the estimation of
learned and devout Hindus, as of sacred origin, and
because it deals far more than any other ancient
book with questions affecting the structure of society
in its minute details. It has had a powerful influence
on the sentiments and habits of the people, such as
the Vedas, even, have probably never had. It stands
as one of the four books of the world that have done
this to an extraordinary degree—the Pentateuch to
the . Jews, the New Testament to Christians, the
Koran to Mahomedans, and Manu to Hindus.

---

[1] 'A code is never the work of a single age, some of the earliest and
rudest laws being preserved, and incorporated with the improvements
of the most enlightened times.' This code is not to be regarded as
'drawn up for the regulation of a particular state under the sanction of
a government. It seems rather to be the work of a learned man,
designed to set forth his ideas of a perfect commonwealth under Hindu
institutions. It may be presumed to reflect the spirit and sentiments of
some ages prior to that of the compiler as well as of his own, and thus
viewed it is of the highest value. Its statements relating to women
are very copious, and whilst some of them are just and humane, others
of them are simply detestable.'—Elphinstone's *History of India*,
Book I.

It is also remarkable that, whilst many of the laws and usages of the Code have become obsolete—if, indeed, some of them were ever anything more than counsels of perfection—and the penalties for violations of the laws and usages can no longer be enforced, the spirit of the Code and its prevailing sentiments survive to this day, and powerfully influence the social and domestic life of the people.

The passages here cited are by no means all that relate to our subject. Some are too offensive for citation, and I have hesitated to insert some which here have a place. It is as repellent a task to quote such sentiments as it will be to read them. But it is advisable that they should be known, and even carefully studied.

It is too much the habit of our age to think favourably of all the religious systems of the East, and of the usages which have sprung from them. Notwithstanding the unutterable filth and intolerable drivel pervading much Hindu literature, it is important that English women should know what the sages and legislators of India have taught relative to the nature, position, and duties of women. It would give them a new and glorious conception of the blessings Christianity has conferred on their sex ; and if they could adequately understand, not only that which Hindu writings of the highest repute teach regarding women, but their position, principally through the powerful influence of those writings, it would rouse their indignation, pity, and zeal in behalf of their

Hindu sisters, as *Uncle Tom's Cabin* did against
slavery in the United States. Here is some of the
evidence in proof of this, and much more will be
given in subsequent pages.

The Code declares—

'It is the nature of women to seduce men in this
world ; for that reason the wise are never unguarded
in the company of females.' [1]

'For women are able to lead astray in this world
not only a fool, but even a learned man, and to make
him a slave of anger and desire.'

'One should not sit in a lonely place with one's
mother, sister, or daughter, for the senses are powerful, and master even a learned man' (chap. ii. 213–215).

'A shepherd, a keeper of buffaloes, the husband of
a remarried woman, and a carrier of dead bodies,—all
these must be carefully avoided.'

'A present to a Brahmin born of a remarried
woman resembles an oblation thrown into ashes '—
distinct condemnations of widow remarriage (chap.
iii. 166, 181).

'Hear now the duties of women. By a girl, by a
young woman, or even by an aged one, nothing must
be done independently, even in her own house.'

'She must not seek to separate herself from her
father, her husband, or sons ; by leaving them she
would make both her own and her husband's families
contemptible.'

---

[1] *The Laws of Manu*, translated by G. Bühler. Published by
Trübner & Co.

'Him to whom her father may give her, or her brother with the father's permission, she shall obey as long as he lives, and when he is dead she must not insult his memory.'

'Though destitute of virtue, or seeking pleasure elsewhere, or devoid of good qualities, yet a husband must be constantly worshipped as a god by a faithful wife.'

'No sacrifice, no vow, no fast must be performed by women apart from their husbands ; if a wife obey her husband, she will for that reason alone be exalted in heaven.'

'A faithful wife, who desires to dwell after death with her husband, must never do anything that would displease him who took her hand, whether he be alive or dead.'

'At her pleasure let her emaciate her body by living on pure flowers, roots, and fruits, but she must never even mention the name of another man after her husband has died.'

'A virtuous wife who after the death of her husband constantly remains chaste, reaches heaven though she have no son.'

'But a woman who from a desire to have offspring violates her duty toward her deceased husband, brings on herself disgrace in this world and loses her place with her husband in heaven.'

'Offspring by another man is here not considered lawful, nor is a second husband anywhere prescribed for virtuous women ' (chap. v. 154–166).

'One man who is free from covetousness may be accepted as virtuous, but not even many pure women, because the understanding of females is apt to waver.'

'No crime, causing loss of caste, is committed by swearing falsely to women' (chap. viii. 70, 77, 112).

'Day and night, women must be kept in dependence by the males of their families.

' Her father protects her in childhood, her husband in youth, and her sons in old age. A woman is never fit for independence.'

'Women must be particularly guarded against evil inclinations, however trifling they may appear, for if they are not guarded they will bring sorrow on two families.'

'When creating them Manu allotted to them a love of their bed, of their seat, and of ornaments, impure desires, wrath, dishonesty, malice, and bad conduct.'

'Knowing their disposition to evil which the Lord of Creatures laid in them at the creation to be such, every man should most strenuously exert himself to guard them.'

'For women no sacramental rite is performed with sacred texts, thus the law is settled ; women who are destitute of strength and of the knowledge of Vedic texts are as impure as falsehood itself, that is a fixed rule.'

'And to this effect many sacred texts are sung

also in the Vedas, in order to make fully known the true disposition of women.'

' On women, infants, men of disordered minds, the poor and the sick, the king shall inflict punishment with a whip, a cane, a rope, and the like.'

' Women, being weak creatures, have no share in the Mantras '—the sacred invocations (chap. ix. 2, 5–18).

' A wife who is barren may be superseded by another in the eighth year ; she whose children are dead in the tenth ; she who brings forth only daughters in the eleventh ; but she who speaks to her husband unkindly may be superseded without delay.'

' She who shows disrespect to a husband, who is addicted to some evil passion, is a drunkard or diseased, shall be deserted for three months, and be deprived of her ornaments and furniture ' (chap. ix. 77–81).

' Stealing grain, base metals or cattle ; slaying women, Sudras, Vaisyas, or Khetriyas '—the inferior castes—' and Atheism, are all minor offences ' (chap. xi. 67).

' A wife is the marital property of her husband.'

' Let the husband neither eat with his wife, nor look at her eating.'

There are a few texts which refer to women in kindlier accents, and their existence along with similar diversity on other questions, lends force to the theory that the Code is an ancient compilation from yet more ancient and various sources. One evidence of this is its lack of coherent statement. The honour, for instance, given in the following texts to mothers contrasts with the disdain generally shown toward women and even wives, though it exhibits the intense desire for sons.

'By honouring his mother he gains the terrestrial world, by honouring his father the ethereal—intermediate—and by assiduous attention to his preceptor, even the celestial world of Brahma.'

'All duties are completely performed by that man by whom these three are completely honoured ; but to him by whom they are dishonoured all other acts are fruitless.'

'So long as these three live, he must perform no other duty for his own sake, but delighting in what may conciliate their affections, and gratify their wishes, he must from day to day assiduously wait on them ' (chap. ii. 233–237).

'Where the female relatives live in grief, the family soon wholly perishes, but that family where they are not unhappy ever prospers.'

'Hence men who seek their own welfare should always honour women on holidays and festivals with gifts of ornaments, clothes, and dainty food.'

'Women must be honoured and adorned by their fathers, brothers, husbands and brothers-in-law who desire their own welfare.'

'Where women are honoured, there the gods are pleased ; but where they are not honoured, no sacred rites yield reward.'

'Where female relatives are made miserable, the family of him who makes them so very soon wholly perishes; but where they are not unhappy, the family always increases.'

'On whatever houses the women of a family, not being duly honoured, pronounce an imprecation, those houses, with all that belong to them, utterly perish as if destroyed by a sacrifice for the death of an enemy.'

'Let these women therefore be continually supplied with ornaments, apparel, and food at festivals and at jubilees by men desirous of wealth.'

'In whatever family the husband is contented with his wife, and the wife with her husband, in that house will good fortune be permanent' (chap. iii. 55–63).

Whilst the Code enjoins respect and honourable treatment to women, its general tendency is to regard them as essentially inferior and subordinate to men. According to it the sexes are not equal ; the woman was made for the man, and is not his companion, but his adjunct, his subordinate, his satellite. Her most religious duty is to serve and obey.

She, like the lower castes, is not fit to be entrusted with the most sacred knowledge.

She is intellectually and morally the inferior of man, therefore she must always be subordinate to him, or through lack of intelligence and virtue she will 'behave amiss.' Her sole use and destiny is to be a wife and mother, and apart from these she has no place or use in life.

These are inferences obviously deduced from the Code. Ample evidence of this is seen in the manners and customs affecting the status of women, in history, and in the various citations that will be found throughout subsequent chapters from various sources.

HINDU WOMAN OF HIGH CASTE.

CHAPTER II.

IT is a remarkable fact, illustrative of the wide difference between Eastern and Western races, that no
Hindu writer has ever given in chronological scientific
order, free from legend and myth, a history of any
race, or, as Tacitus, Macaulay, and Green, a portraiture
of the ordinary life of a people, with their manners,
customs, and conditions of life.

Hindu writings are more numerous and varied than
those of any other ancient race, but in many of them,
as the Puranas and Great Epics, history, biography,
and philosophic speculation are so intermingled with
mythology, legend, supernaturalism and extravagance,
that the facts and truths to be gleaned from them,
after careful sifting and analysis, are comparatively
few.

The most ancient and revered of the Hindu scriptures take us back to times probably contemporaneous
with those of the Judges and earlier Kings of Israel,
and present to us a picture of society not greatly

different from that of Syria and Palestine. It was
simple, fairly well organized, and religious. Bar-
barians there were, but the ruling, dominant race,
the Aryans, the ancestors of the Hindus, were neither
ignorant nor barbarous, as judged by the standard of
ancient times. Society was organized and graded.
The people could move and act in the mass and in
concert. They obeyed constituted authorities, recog-
nizing the force and reasonableness of certain laws,
usages, and principles. They were as a race united
and strong. They acknowledged divine power and
authority. They believed and worshipped, if not
as correctly as the Patriarchs, yet far more so than
the vast bulk of their descendants in the present
day.

In philosophy, astronomy, poetry, and all the arts
of civilization they were far in advance of the aboriginal
inhabitants of India, whom they, therefore, easily dis-
placed or reduced to subjection.

The status of women corresponded with all this ;
and in considering what it was, and, indeed, what it is
now, the fact should be kept in mind, that no Asiatic
race in any period of history has ever given to women
that place which Western races, and especially Protestant nations, give them.

In the Vedic period of Indian history, which takes
us back to times antecedent to Manu's Code, women
were in as favourable a position as they were anywhere in ancient times. Honour, respect, confidence,
and liberty were freely accorded to them. Marriages

were free from almost all the usages which have degraded them in recent times. Monogamy was the general rule of married life, but polygamy was not unknown,[1] neither was polyandry. But in these early ages we find no instances of child marriage, enforced widowhood, and contempt and distrust of women, so common in subsequent times.

Following the earliest ages of Hindu society, there come times less simple and tranquil, and more legendary. The position of women during those times was materially altered. The two great Indian epics, the Ramayan and Mahabharat, portions of which have even now an extraordinary influence over the imaginations and thoughts of the people, present to us few detailed and minute descriptions of domestic life, or of the relative position of the two sexes among the great masses of the people; but make it clear that the women of the upper ranks of society had much more freedom than the same class now. Their wishes and desires were more consulted, and their appearance in public was allowed, and probably welcomed. At all events, when there were great gatherings on festival occasions, or for the display of prowess, skill, and courage analogous to the tournaments of the ages of chivalry, whilst there were galleries for men who were spectators and combatants, there were others for their wives and daughters, who came to add by their presence and the splendour of their array to its attractiveness, to stimulate the

[1] *Teaching of the Vedas*, by the Rev. Maurice Phillips.

combatants not only by their presence, but their gestures and utterances. The general condition of all classes of women must have been far higher than it has ever been since, when one class at least, and that the highest, was thus honoured and free.

One usage then was permissible, which would be impossible where modern Hindu sentiment relative to women is prevalent—the Swayamvara, or self-choice, when a maiden of high rank selected for herself a husband either purely by choice, or through some test of courage or skill. Such cases, no doubt, were rare, but they sufficiently justify the inference we have drawn. In confirmation of this we recall the exquisite episode of Nala and Damayanti, as an instance of such usage, which amply sustains this opinion, as the words following will show :—

' Bhima, the Rajah of Vidarbha, sent to all neighbouring countries to proclaim in behalf of his daughter a Swayamvara. Many came, allured by the report of her exceeding loveliness. Among them was Nala, King of Nashadha. He entered the palace, saw Damayanti, and conversed with her. On the great day of selection all the rajahs crowded to the palace, and when Damayanti entered every soul was entranced at her dazzling beauty. Soon the name of each rajah was proclaimed aloud, and Damayanti glanced around at the glittering throng. At length, spying the object of her affections, in all maidenly modesty she went up to him, and taking hold of the hem of his robe and casting a wreath of flowers on his neck, thus chose him as her lord. A sound of wild sorrow bursts from all the rajahs. But Nala turned to the slender-waisted maiden and said, 'Since, O maiden with the eye serene, you have chosen me for your husband, know that I will be your faithful consort, ever delighting in your words; and as long as my soul shall inherit this body I solemnly vow to be yours and yours alone.'

The story of Ram and Sita, which forms the basis of the Ramayan, is almost unequalled as a record of affection and fidelity between husband and wife, in spite of extraordinary trials. The two are the ideals of manhood and womanhood, and of mutual love and loyalty in the heroic periods of Hindu history: Ram, the ideal of noble self-denial, honour, courage, and endurance; Sita, of submission to her husband's will and fortunes, of chastity and fidelity. The conception, however, of the subordination of the wife to the husband runs through the marvellous romance. Nevertheless, it is honourable to Hindu intelligence and virtue that for so many centuries the Ramayan has so profoundly won the respect and admiration of all who have any claim to education or refinement.

In one of the hymns of the Rig Veda there is an allusion to the 'husband of many maidens.' In another a Rishi praises the generosity of a rajah for having given him in marriage his ten daughters. In another the Aswins, twin brothers, are thus congratulated: 'Aswins, your admirable horses bore the car which you had harnessed first to the jail for

C

the sake of honour ; and the damsel who was the prize came to you and acknowledged your husband-ship, saying, " You are my lords." '

According to established usage the eldest brother was entitled as a matter of right to select and marry a damsel, who then became the joint wife of himself and his younger brethren. So clear and indisputable was this right held to be, that it might override and supersede the prior right acquired by the victor at a Swayamvara. Of this we have a signal exemplification in the case of Draupadi, who became beyond all question or dispute the lawful prize of Arguna, one of the younger of the five Pandava brothers. But by the decision of the Divine Sage, Vyasa, and with the full and harmonious consent of all the parties chiefly interested, the superior right of Yudhisthira, the eldest brother, was with due formality conceded. Thereupon Draupadi was first married to him, and afterwards successively to the others according to their relative ages.

Nor is it to be supposed that this marriage of Draupadi to the five sons of Raja Pandu is an isolated event, which might have been surreptitiously inter-polated in the stirring narrative of the Great War. It is enwoven as an integral and constituent element into its very texture ; it is one of the main hinges on which the plot of the terrible tragedy of the war is made to turn, and ever and anon it comes to the forefront of the unfolding roll of its marvellous scenes and soul-stirring incidents.

Contrasting the present with the past, it is clear that formerly women were then more respected and trusted. If not regarded as equal to men, they stood nearer to them in general estimation for virtue and intelligence. Education, accomplishments, and influence were open to them. Their power was felt in the family, the tribe, public affairs, and literature. Dr. Wilson of Bombay declared that ' in no nation of antiquity were women held in so much esteem as among the Hindus,' and the most ancient religious, philosophical, and literary writings give colour to this opinion ; and certainly in those ancient records there is no evidence of the systematic and all-prevailing degradation to which the whole sex has been doomed for some centuries.

HINDU WOMEN CARRYING WATER.

CHAPTER III.

THAT the more kindly sentiments and opinions expressed in the latter quotations from the Code of Manu have, in all ages, prevailed in many families, is undoubted. Good sense, natural affection, humanity and gentleness are qualities in which Hindus are certainly not lacking ; and that, under the influence of Christian teaching and example, they are gaining the mastery over superstition and prejudice is gladly recognized. But now we have to indicate the authoritative and prevalent drift of native opinion and sentiment. And this is the more important, since written and public opinion has in all ages governed the conduct and shaped the policy of the people, to a degree most marked and significant. Two sources of authority will assist us here : the Gentoo Code, and common proverbs and sayings.

This Code is a most interesting and significant expression of native law and sentiment, and reveals what, towards the close of last century, these were, according to the highest living authorities; and as it is largely based on Manu's Code, it justifies the inference that all through the intervening centuries the low and contemptuous conceptions of women's abilities, character, and status disclosed in the earlier Code had been dominant.

The origin of this Code is interesting, and is given in the preface, written by N. Brassey Halhed, who translated it from Persian into English at the instance of Warren Hastings, in 1775. This was its origin. As soon as the East India Company became rulers in India they were under the necessity of administering law and justice, and were soon made conscious of the wide difference between English and Hindu and Mahomedan law; of the necessity of paying much attention to the latter, and of their own ignorance of its principles and details. To assist them 'a number of the most experienced lawyers were selected by the Government in Calcutta from every part of Bengal, for the purpose of compiling the Code, which they picked out sentence by sentence from various originals in the Sanscrit language, neither adding to nor diminishing any part of the sacred texts. The articles thus collected were next translated into Persian—at that time the language of the law courts —under the inspection of one of their own body, and from that translations were rendered into English, with an equal attention to the closeness and fidelity of the version. From hence, therefore, may be formed a precise idea of the customs and manners of these people, who, to their great injury, have long been misrepresented in the Western world.'

The immutability of the East is seen in the fact that, after more than 1200 years, the sentiments prevalent throughout Hindu society relating to women, and the customs defining their position, correspond with those expressed in Manu. The one Code is the echo of the other. Just as a river running through a mountainous and rocky district abides in the same channel age after age, deepening its bed, it may be, but never leaving it, so the sentiments enunciated by the great codifier have all through the long interval operated on society almost as a law of nature does on physical elements. Abundant evidence of the close correspondence between ancient and recent times will be observed in the following extracts from the Gentoo Code :—

'A man both day and night must keep his wife so much in subjection that she by no means becomes mistress of her own actions. If the wife have her own free will, notwithstanding she be sprung from a superior caste, she will yet behave amiss.'

'Women have six qualities : an inordinate desire for jewels and fine furniture, handsome clothes and nice victuals ; inordinate desire ; violent anger ; deep resentment ; another person's good appears evil in their eyes ; they commit bad actions.'

'A woman shall never go out of the house without the consent of her husband.'

'A woman shall never go to a stranger's house,

and shall never stand at the door, and must never look out of a window.   She must not eat till she has served her husband and his guests with food.'

'It is proper for a woman, after her husband's death, to burn herself in the fire with his corpse; every woman who thus burns herself shall remain in Paradise with her husband threescore and fifty laks of years' (3,500,000).

Thus were the degrading, pernicious sentiments of the ancient Code accepted and endorsed by great legal authorities toward the close of last century. And there is ample evidence that both express the opinions prevalent at least for several centuries.   The customs and usages which will be considered in some subsequent chapters offer ample evidence of this; and so do the following extracts from two most diverse sources—the leaders of opinion on all questions of philosophy, morals, and religion, and the common proverbs and sayings of the people.   The following quotations could be extended indefinitely, but they are sufficient as evidence, and the writer may well be spared the pain of adding to them, and the reader the indignation they excite.

'Let the husband be choleric and dissipated, irregular, a drunkard, a gambler, a debauchee; suppose him reckless of domestic affairs, agitated like a demon; let him live in the world destitute of honour; let him be deaf or blind; his crimes and infirmities may weigh him down, but never shall his wife regard him but as her god' (*Padma Purana*).

'When in the presence of her husband, a woman must not look on one side or the other; she must keep her eyes on her master, to be ready to receive his commands. Her husband may sometimes be in a passion; he may threaten her, he may use imperious language, he may unjustly beat her, but under no circumstances shall she make any return but meek and soothing words' (*Padma Purana*).

'A father secures the safety of a woman in infancy, a husband in youth, children in old age, but a woman who follows her own inclination cannot be secured from sin or folly' (*Hitōpodesh*).

'The beauty of a cocil bird is its song; the beauty of a woman is obedience to her husband' (*Hitōpodesh*).

'Should her husband call, even though she were eating ambrosia, she should joyfully quit it and hasten to him' (*Casi Candam*).

'Let the wife who wishes to perform a sacred ablution, wash the feet of her lord and drink the water; for a husband is to a wife greater than Shantiara (an eminent sage) or Vishnu.'

'Her husband is her god and guru, teacher and guide, and religion and its services; wherefore, abandoning everything else, she ought chiefly to worship her husband' (*The Skanda Purana*, cited by Horace Hayman Wilson).

'To well-born women their husband is a god.'

'Though her husband be of surpassing beauty, youthful, powerful in song, of an aspect to ravish the eyes of maidens, and uniting truth with courtesy in

his pleasing address, the heart of woman will still be
fixed on others' (*Nithi Valaccam*).

'They are void of the feelings of honour ; regard-
less of pride of birth ; their minds are ever vacant ;
they have a thousand varying wills' (*Sinthamani*).

'It is impossible to restrain within any bounds
those who are adorned with jewels—women—if they
are devoid of good qualities. Shall I say why? Is it
possible by any means, or by binding it ever so tightly,
to keep a dog's tail straight? No!' (*Parlyamarlyi*).

'In creatures with nails, in rivers, in horned
animals, in those with weapons in their hands, confidence must not be placed ; nor in women, nor in
kings' favourites. One may trust deadly poison ; a
river ; a hurricane ; the beautiful, large, fierce elephant ;
the tiger come for prey ; the Angel of Death ; a thief ;
a savage ; a murderer ; but if one trust a woman,
without doubt he must wander about in the streets
as a beggar.'

It may be supposed by some who are ignorant of
Hindu literature, or who desire to think favourably
of Hinduism, that we have cited only its unfavourable
features. They are such, at least, as are most prevalent.
This is the testimony of a most competent witness.
The Pundita Ramabai Sarasati, in her *High Caste
Hindu Women*, says : 'I can honestly say, and truth-
fully, that I have never read any sacred book in
Sanscrit literature without meeting with a low and
degrading conception of the character and influence
of women.'

The sentiment at the root of all domestic life is that women have neither sufficient intelligence nor moral strength nor sense of honour to protect themselves, and need, therefore, as much to be guarded from themselves as from others. And this demoralizes and injures alike the men who cherish such sentiments and the women who have to endure the wrong. 'Woman,' wrote Dr. William Arthur, 'is, according to Hindu masculine sentiment, a compound of all the vices. The following passage, cited by Mill, accurately expresses (notwithstanding the remarks of Professor H. H. Wilson) the estimate of woman generally given by the people in familiar conversation : " Infidelity, violence, deceit, envy, extreme avariciousness, a total want of good qualities, with impurity, are the innate faults of womankind." " To teach a woman," they have said to me, " would be to give a serpent milk ; she would turn her knowledge into venom." And again, " Keep women at what distance we may, it is hard to govern them ; but did we make them our equals, teaching them to read and write, farewell to the hope of ruling our houses."

'Even the nobles in the court of Ahasuherus were not more jealous than the meanest Hindu of the right of men to bear rule in their own house. They profess great alarm for the moral consequences of female education, asking, " If it be almost impossible, in the present state of things, to preserve a family from intrigues, how would it be if the women could send and receive notes ? " The connection that has

long existed between an educated and a disreputable
woman enlists the prejudices even of the women
themselves against their own education. A respectable man said to me, " The most fatal error one
can commit is to treat his wife affectionately ; from
the day he exhibits tenderness towards her, his
independence and his peace are gone. She will dread
him no longer. All the vices of her nature will break
forth ; his home is no more his own, and he must
bear with her tongue and temper all his days. If,"
added he, "you bear affection to a parent, a brother,
a child, or even a servant, you may display it ; but
if you love your wife, you must never allow her to
suspect it is so, or farewell to peace." [1]

The following incident is no doubt exceptional,
but the sentiments expressed are by no means so.
A man was brought before Sir Charles Napier,
charged with killing his wife in a fit of rage. With his
usual promptitude, the guilt of the man being proved,
as well as the innocence of the wife, Sir Charles
sentenced the man to be hung forthwith. On learning this, a native of rank belonging to a warlike race,
exclaimed, ' What ! you will hang a man for *only*
killing his wife ? ' ' Yes,' replied Sir Charles ; ' she
had done no wrong.' ' Wrong ! No ; but he was
angry : why should he not kill her ? '

Mr. Dutt, a member of an influential and gifted
family in Bengal, says, ' The position of women in
India has hitherto been one of degradation and

[1] *Mission to the Mysore.*

servitude. Though the legislators of Hindustan have not, in common with the sterner lawgiver of the Mahomedans, excluded females from Paradise, nor denied that they have souls, they have treated them in every respect with marked indignity and contempt, sparing no occasion to give vent to their scorn. While the minutest provisions are made in the Shastras for the mental cultivation of the boys, not even one stray text is to be found advocating the instruction of female children. On the contrary, women are in many places expressly refused access to the sacred scriptures of the country, and prohibited the acquirement of literary instruction, under a curse. The female who can read and write is branded as the heir of misfortunes. The Vedas are not even to be heard by women. And from the other sources of information they are also debarred ; as, according to the authorities most commonly known and revered, the study of letters is considered a disqualification for domestic usefulness, and the sure, inevitable harbinger of danger and distress. Women have accordingly received no education in this country, neither in childhood nor in youth, much less in maturer years.

'Nor is this all ; not satisfied with debarring woman from mental cultivation, the lawgivers of India have also imputed unto her many of the worst propensities of human nature, and to her conduct attributed all the miseries of human life. All the invective that wit could devise, all the sarcasm that her sex could countenance, have been used, bitterly and brutally, against her to injure her reputation. "Woman," say the Gentoo laws, "is never satisfied with the gratification of her appetites, no more than fire is satisfied with burning fuel, or the main ocean with receiving the rivers." Manu also tells us that women are always ready to corrupt men, whether wise or foolish. In the same strain says the Nit Shaster—"To lie, to be impudent, to deceive, to speak bitter words, to be unclean and cruel, are all vices inherent in woman's nature, and most of all to find fault with a man, if her wishes are not satisfied."

'And the Vedas declare woman to be an incarnation of sin. In the works of some of the sages and poets, though they all generally teem with the most wicked misrepresentations of her character, there are indeed some portraits in which she has also been delineated as amiable, modest, and high-principled ; but we are not speaking now of the occasional opinions of isolated admirers, but of the notions entertained on the subject by the community at large. The nations of antiquity, one and all, appear to have held woman in disesteem ; and the more corrupt the character of the people, the greater the share of their contempt for the sex. Nowhere has the national character ever been more low than in India, and nowhere was a worse opinion of female integrity generally entertained.'[1]

The same low conceptions of women find expression in the common proverbs and sayings.

[1] *Essays*, by Shoshi Chunder Dutt, p. 267. Calcutta.

' Do not listen to the words of your wife.'

'The man who acts not according to his own opinion, but according to that of his wife, cannot discharge the necessary duties connected with this world or the world to come.' These are the sentiments of Ouvay, a Tamil lady, the most popular and renowned authoress India has ever produced. Thus writing, she expressed, we may assume, not her own convictions, but the prevalent ideas, for it has ever been a characteristic of the Hindu race to keep within the limits of surrounding thought and action.

' Ignorance is an ornament to women.'

' A drum, a rustic, a servant, a woman—all these go on right when struck.'

' A woman's will no one knows ; after killing her husband, she will herself become suttee.'

' He who listens to the words of a woman will be accounted worthless.'

' Even were a woman well read and learned, taking her counsel would lead to the eating of refuse.'

'Sickness is caused by water, sin by woman.'

' A tree on the bank of a river, wealth in another man's possession, a matter known to a woman,—all these must be fruitless.'

' Women are as unsteady as the birds that float in the air.'

' Never put your trust in woman—woman's counsel leads to destruction.'

' Woman is a great whirlpool of suspicion, a

dwelling-place of vices, full of deceits, a hindrance
in the way of heaven, the gate of hell.'

One of the peculiarities of the cocoanut palm is
that it seldom stands upright. A Malayan saying has
it that, ' He who has looked upon a dead monkey,
he who has found the nest of the paddy-bird, he
who hath beheld a straight cocoanut, or has fathomed
the deceitful heart of woman, will live for ever.'

The following quotation is given as a specimen of
the teaching set forth in a book which was distributed
broadcast as a prize-book in the Government girls'
schools in the Bombay Presidency :—

' If the husband of a virtuous woman be ugly, of
good or bad disposition, diseased, fiendish, irascible,
a drunkard, old, stupid, dumb, blind, deaf, hot-
tempered, poor, extremely covetous, a slanderer,
cowardly, perfidious, and immoral, nevertheless she
ought to worship him as a god, with mind, speech,
and person. The wife who gives an angry answer to
her husband will become a village pariah dog ; she
will also become a female jackal, and live in an
uninhabited desert. The woman who eats sweetmeats without sharing them with her husband will
become a hen-owl living in a hollow tree. The
woman who walks alone without her husband will
become a filth-eating village sow. The woman who
speaks disrespectfully to her husband will be dumb
in the next incarnation. The woman who hates her
husband's relatives will become from birth to birth a
musk rat living in filth.'

A Sanscrit Catechism reads thus—
  'What is cruel?
  The heart of a viper.
  What is more cruel than that?
  The heart of a woman.
  What is the cruellest of all?
  The heart of a soulless widow.'
Another Catechism or Manual reads thus—
  'What is the chief gate to hell?
  A woman.
  What bewitches like wine?
  A woman.
  Who is the wisest of the wise?
  He who has not been deceived by woman, who
    may be compared to malignant fiends.
  Who are fetters to men?
  Women.
  What is that which cannot be trusted?
  Women.
  What poison is that which appears like nectar?
  A woman.'

'Blind sons support their parents, but a prince's daughter extorts money from them.'

That is, a son, however helpless, will care for his parents, but a daughter, however rich, will try to get all she can from hers.

'Unless a daughter dies, she cannot be praised for her virtues.'

Women are so fickle and frail that you are never sure what their lives will turn out to be.

'Those who attend to the words of a woman are possessed with devils.'

'Females produce young ones. They are given to exaggeration, and produce wonderful stories out of very meagre facts.'

'We cannot understand the character of women. Even the gods cannot.'

In South India the following story is told in praise of the abject submission to her husband on the part of a wife. Valluvar, a sage, was asked by a disciple which was best, a married or unmarried state. He told his disciple to wait for an answer, and one day when he was present called his wife Vasugi, who was in the act of drawing water from a deep well, who instantly left the vessel suspended halfway and ran to him. On another occasion when she was giving him cold rice, he said, ' This is burning me,' when instantly she ran for a fan and fanned him. Then, when weaving at noonday, he dropped his shuttle, and calling to his wife for a light, she immediately brought one. Then said the sage to the disciple, ' If such an obedient one can be found, it is good to marry, but not otherwise.'

The Arabs say—and their literature and sentiments have spread over Western Asia and Northern Africa —that the wicked one thus addressed woman at the creation : 'Thou art half of my host, and thou art the depositary of my secret, and thou art my arrow with which I shoot, and miss not.'

Mahomed is reported to have said, ' I stood at

the gate of hell, and lo, most of the inmates were women!'

The Caliph Abu Bekr said, 'The women are all evil, but the greatest evil of all is that they are necessary.'

Another caliph, Omar, said, 'Consult them, and do the contrary to what they advise.'

Jewish literature and ceremonialism exhibit the same features. According to Maimonides there are ten sorts of persons disqualified to give evidence in a court of justice. These are women, slaves, children, idiots, the deaf, blind, wicked, despised, relatives, and those interested in a case. The devout Jew in his prayers says, 'Blessed art Thou, O Lord God, King of the Universe, who hast not made me a woman.' The Jewess meekly prays, 'Blessed art Thou, O Lord God, King of the Universe, who hast made me according to Thy will.' She is not allowed to take part in worship on the floor of the synagogue, but with her sex apart, behind the lattice-work, seeing, but not seen, a silent worshipper, for it is not permitted her to join vocally in the service.

But nobler sentiments are not wanting. For instance—

'God did not make woman from man's head, that she should rule over him, nor from his feet, that she should be his slave, but from his side, that she should be near his heart' (*Talmud*).

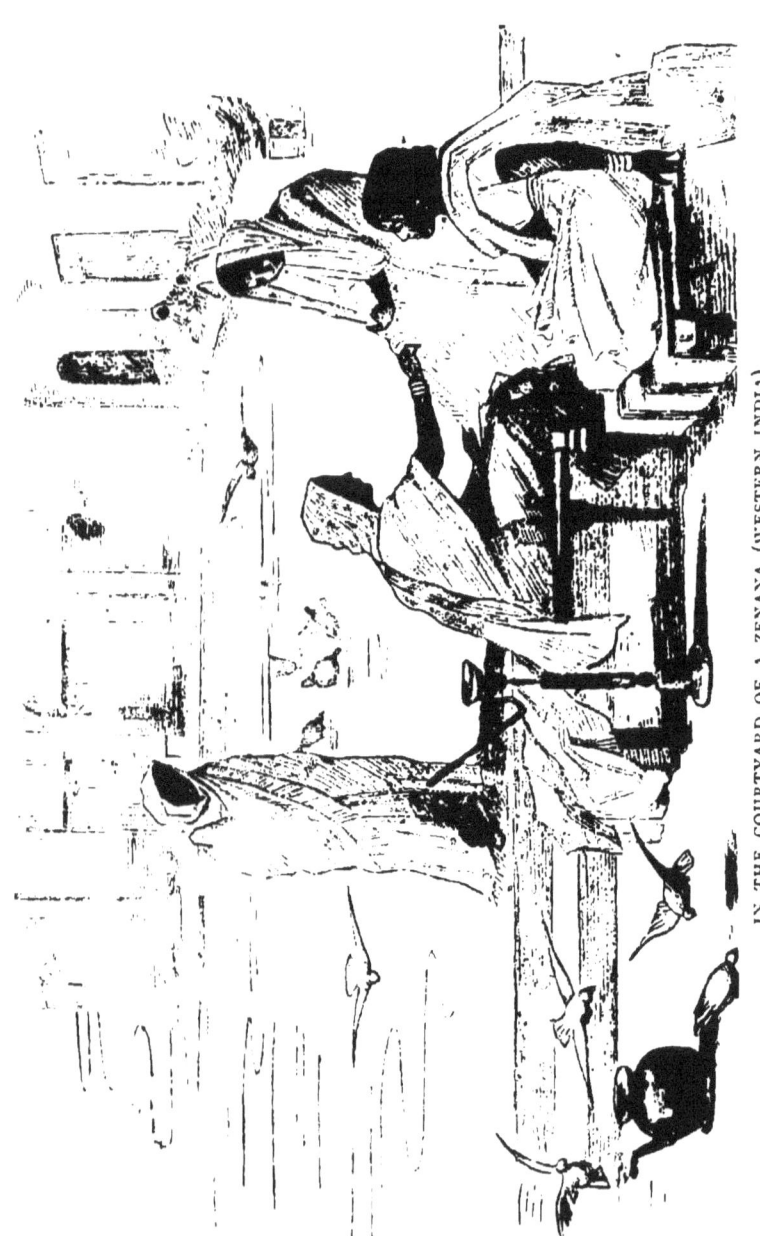

IN THE COURTYARD OF A ZENANA (WESTERN INDIA).

A HINDU MEAL.

CHAPTER IV.

DAILY LIFE.

HINDU dwellings indicate by their form the in-security of former ages, the suspicion and distrust yet prevalent, and the great social differences existing between men and women. Every Hindu aims to secure privacy and seclusion in his dwelling. He likes his house to be separate from others ; to surround it with a wall or hedge ; to be embosomed in trees and shrubs, and to be free from the observation of neighbours.

Almost every house is the property of the family inhabiting it. They are usually small, with one room, or at the most two. The sides consist of mats, or wickerwork between posts, or of earth formed into low walls, or sun-dried bricks. The roof is very low-pitched, and composed of straw, reeds, palm leaves, or tiles, so small and light that crows often displace them. The interior is bare and gloomy, for there is no window, though there may be a small wooden lattice ; and in front, to the south, if practicable, a small raised platform, protected by the overhanging roof from the sun and rain. A mat may be on a part of the mud floor. There are no chairs, drawers, or table, but a box, a few coarse earthen vessels for oil, water, and cooking, and a charpoy, which serves as a bedstead and lounge. The fireplace consists of three or four bricks or stones, but there is no chimney, the smoke finding its way out of the roof as best it can.

Probably nine-tenths of the families in India live in such houses. But there is far less discomfort in them than those unfamiliar with India would suppose. The intense heat causes fires to be unnecessary except for cooking, shoes and stockings to be an encum-brance, body and bed clothing to be of the lightest, and sleeping out in the open air on most nights a pleasure rather than an inconvenience.

But houses of a better class most truly express the Hindu ideal. They, too, stand apart, and usually have a bare, forbidding appearance. The side walls are of coarse brick or bare masonry, with no outlook. The roof is usually flat. On entering the small well-protected door, you pass into a court open to the sky. On either side, perhaps also over the entrance, runs a narrow verandah communicating with small, ill-ventilated, badly lighted rooms. Opposite the door on the fourth side is a raised platform, appropriated to religious uses. Here the images of the gods are placed, and the paraphernalia of worship, and at the great religious festivals, sacrifices and worship are celebrated in the presence of spectators in the court-yard and the surrounding verandahs. At the back of this, communicating with it by a small door, is the women's part of the house, the zenana, constructed somewhat as the front portion, but smaller and with an eye to greater seclusion. At the back of this, again, is often a well-enclosed garden, in which is a tank, so that the ladies and children may bathe and take exercise unseen and undisturbed.

The inhabitants of such houses are usually far more numerous than in any ordinary European family, are more subject to precedent and authority, and live more apart from their neighbours.

It is regarded as a matter of course that sons and daughters are married at a very early age. Equally is it regarded as a matter of course that sons with their wives and children shall live in the family house, not as separate entities, but an integral part of the family or commonwealth. It is a binding obligation on every head of a family to provide for all the distressed, helpless, and unemployed of his kith and kin. The claim is often a wide one, and if the head of the family or even some of its subordinate members, are in fair circumstances, it is surprising what a number of poor relatives may lay claim 'to bed and board.' The claims are generally allowed with the utmost politeness, though made by the idle and worthless, and in many cases sadly weigh on the family resources. But custom sanctions the usage, and nothing must therefore be said. Then, too, since widows in such families do not marry, they and their children help to increase the number of inhabitants in a father or father-in-law's household.

From these various causes it happens that families are often very large, consisting of twenty-five, fifty, one hundred, and even more relatives, including not only parents and children, but brothers and sisters-in-law, uncles and aunts, and cousins of all degrees. Whatever money is gained is put into the common purse, held by the father, or, if he has passed away, by the elder brother. The position of family head is a real, not a nominal one. He is an autocrat whose will is law. So is it on the female side of the house, the two sexes living apart.

It would be regarded as improper, and subject a

man to ridicule and contempt, if he were to eat with his wife or any other woman, or converse with them on terms of equality. Nor is there any ordinary occasion when the male and female members of the family come together. There is no dining, drawing, sitting-room, or parlour free to men and women alike. Even on occasions when husbands and wives meet before others, it is considered good form for the husband to refrain from all expressions of affection or partiality for his wife. She too must not sit in his presence, unless requested to do so. It is he, not she, who must introduce conversation; it is her part to listen and obey. She must not directly address him by name; to do so would be to degrade him in the presence of onlookers by too great familiarity. If they have a child, the mother speaks of her husband through the child's name as the father of Gopal or of Sita. If they have no child, she uses a respectful personal pronoun equivalent to 'he,' perhaps adding the expression 'mine' or 'ours.' So the husband never pronounces the wife's name. He speaks of her as the mother of so and so, or uses a yet more vague form of expression, literally meaning 'the people of my family,' though generally the allusion is only to the wife. Some ludicrous instances of the former usage occurred when the census was taken, since, in the absence of the husband, wives could not be induced to utter their names, and were too illiterate to write them. The entire demeanour of the wife must be expressive of deference and submission.

The front part of the house, the courtyard, and verandahs are accessible on easy terms to servants and neighbours, but the female side of the house is strictly private, and given over to isolation and monotony. No man must visit there, even though he be an uncle, a brother-in-law, or a cousin. The visits even of female relatives and neighbours are infrequent and formal ; no one older than a mere child must penetrate into the men's side of the house, and only for the sleeping-hours may the men retire to that small portion of the zenana which belongs to the wife. If ladies take a journey or visit their own relatives, every precaution is taken that they may not be seen, though some allowance is made that they may see through the lattices of a carriage or palanquin. If a European visits the house, he will be received with marked courtesy, but an introduction into the zenana or to any adult lady of the family is not to be thought of, though he may surmise that feminine eyes observe him by peeping over the balustrades of the roof, or through jalousies or curtains or other coigns of vantage. As few visits are paid, so few are received, excepting in cases where houses are so near to each other that the inmates may pass and repass over some narrow lane without fear of observation.

The apartments in a zenana are usually bare, dreary, and comfortless to an extreme degree. The walls are neither papered nor painted ; tables, chairs, sofas, drawers, cabinets are seldom seen. The windows and jalousies are small, and constructed so as to give light only; they look into the courtyard or garden, or toward the open country, never into the street, or if they do, they are placed so high that the sky, not the earth, can be seen.

The difficulty of making word-pictures of a zenana vivid is great. Here is a description from a missionary friend who had felt the difficulty. ' I had often wondered why one had such a dim impression of what a zenana was like, and wished for a minute description. I now wonder no longer. A zenana is simply indescribable, from the fact that no two are alike, and not one seems to have been built on any supposable plan or shape. A collection of dirty courtyards, dark corners, breakneck staircases, filthy outhouses and entries, overlaid with rubbish or occupied by half-clad native servants stretched about on charpoys or on the ground; indifferently narrow verandahs, and unfurnished or semi-furnished rooms, and very small; such is a zenana and its surroundings. Very often the approach to the house is so intricate, or rough, or narrow, that it becomes an impossibility for the ghari to approach, and the missionary must go on foot—a perilous proceeding under the scorching rays of a tropical sun. Once inside the zenana, you are struck, as a rule, by the entire absence of all that constitutes to our idea the complement of a room— furniture, tables, and chairs are not to be thought of, *except when brought in from the Babu's apartments*, for the teacher's use for the time being.'

This was written of the Calcutta zenanas. A missionary from Benares writes : ' The homes here are more gloomy, dirty, and devoid of every comfort even than in Calcutta. Even at this cold season the majority of the women wear no other clothing than their thin sarees, and sit on the cold mud or flag floors with their uncovered legs and feet, so that one wonders they are not constantly suffering from rheumatism.' Another writes : ' The women always have the worst part of the house assigned them, and seem to have few comforts given them. Even in the large residences of the rich Babus one can always tell when getting near the rooms allotted to the women by the dirty and miserable appearance of the walls, staircases, and courts. Many of the high-caste natives are very poor, and then they have to live in very small, wretched houses ; but some of them are rich enough, and their dwellings are large and airy, and furnished with luxuries, but the ladies do not share in the comforts, though they may be better dressed, and have more servants to wait on them.'

But what of the dwellers in these cheerless, prison-like abodes ? In natural endowments, Hindu women will compare favourably with their sisters anywhere. Their features are most regular, and often refined and delicate. They lack expression, as might be expected from their want of intellectual training, but gentleness of disposition and physical beauty commonly belong to them. In form they are elegant and

graceful, fit models for any sculptor or painter. They
walk with slow and measured step. Their dress is
simple and suited to their manner of life, usually it
consists of one long piece of light cotton cloth,
wrapped in graceful folds round the body, leaving
one limb partially free ; then from under her arm,
gathering it up in front, she draws it across her
left shoulder and tucks it in above her waist behind.
Usually the upper part rests on her shoulders, but it
can easily be lifted on her head and drawn across
her face, or the whole upper part be lowered to her
waist. This is usually done when she is alone or at
work. Thus the one piece of cloth usually serves as
skirt, jacket, and bonnet. Sometimes a light bodice
with short sleeves is worn.

Next to children, ornaments are the chief joy of
women ; they not only give pleasure to their minds,
untrained to value higher possessions, but are always
regarded as the measure of the family position and
the affection of the husband. Those of the poor are
made of brass, shells, and glass. Those of the rich, of
silver, gold, and precious stones. Their number is
great ; thirty-six distinct kinds may be worn by a
Tamil lady, and often several of the same kind, and the
number worn by ladies in Northern India is almost
as great.

How do they pass their time ? The wives of the
poor and low castes have far more to interest them than
those of higher rank. They go more abroad ; they
see and hear more. The management of domestic

affairs rests with them, and having more freedom, they become more self-reliant and intelligent. They

AT THE RIVERSIDE (ALLAHABAD).

often work hard, have coarse food, few comforts, and are harshly treated. They have daily to bring water

from the well, purchase in the market the necessary
articles, cook the food, attend to the house and
children, and perhaps work in the farm or garden.

Zenana ladies are much more carefully tended, but
their lives are intensely dull, monotonous, and trivial—
so at least they seem to us. They never leave the
house singly or in company for a walk or shopping
or visiting. To do so would be not only ruinous to
the reputation of any zenana lady, but also regarded
as disgraceful to her family.

Visits are rarely paid or received, and then are
arranged with much ceremony. There are multitudes
of ladies who have never enjoyed a free long walk,
or been in any house but their father's and father's-
in-law, or travelled a mile from either, or have the
least idea of the town or village in which they were
born. 'You,' said a young lady in a zenana to an
Englishwoman, pointing to a bird on the wing—'you
are like that bird soaring to heaven ; we are like birds
caught, their wings cut, and shut up in cages too
narrow for them.'

Cooking is the principal event of the day, and is
usually done with great skill and completeness ; but,
since there is but one cooking for the whole family,
and as several members of the family can assist as
well as servants, this occupies no great proportion of
the time. They clean the cooking utensils ; bathe and
dress their children ; dress and braid their hair ; look
at their jewels and the jewels of one another ; eat,
lounge, sleep ; hear the gossip brought in on the

previous night by each husband to his wife and by the servants—and that is all!

What a dull, cheerless, restricted existence theirs is! Some part of each day many English women are left to themselves, but they ever have the consciousness of freedom : they can go out, they receive visits, read, and toward evening the house is made bright and cheerful by the return of the husband and sons ; and the glory and delight of Christian family life is seen in men and women using the same room, sitting around the same table, eating the same food, and conversing freely as equals. Nothing of the kind is seen in India.

This segregation of the sexes in the same family is disastrous alike to men and women, and it is difficult to say which sex is most injuriously affected. What a world of significance is conveyed in the remark that in India there are 'houses, but no homes'! 'We have no homes,' said the Dewan Bahadur R. Raghonath Rao. 'There exists,' writes Sir M. Monier Williams, 'no word that I know of in any Indian language exactly equivalent to that grand old Saxon monosyllable "home"—that little word which is the key to our national greatness and prosperity. Certainly the word "zenana," meaning in Persian "the place of women," cannot pretend to stand for "home," any more than the Persian "mandana," "the place for men," can mean "home." '

In the zenana itself there are abundant sources of discomfort and trouble. Women's sole companions are near relatives, chiefly nieces, aunts, and sisters-in-law, some married, others unmarried, but all confined within the same restricted intellectual, social, and material horizon. However patient, gentle, submissive women may be, it is inevitable that many occasions for envy, jealousy, and discord must exist in families so constituted. There is, indeed, an authority whose will is supreme—the grandmother or mother-in-law or sister-in-law, whose Oriental conception of autocratic power is not likely to be softened by previous subordination, and still less by sweet reasonableness, the discipline of education, or the beneficent influence of a pure religion. Usually delighting in the exercise of power over others, and being ignorant and superstitious, and the most conservative where all are so, she is the enemy of all change and reform. Her government is a pure despotism, all the more harsh and overbearing because it is exercised for the most part over the daughters of other women. Report speaks of this as one of the darkest and saddest features of life in the zenanas, and so do such current sayings as the following :—

'If the mother-in-law break the pan, it is earthen ; if the daughter-in-law, it is golden.'

'Gold answering to the assayer's test and a woman agreeable to her mother-in-law are scarce.'

'Tears come into the eyes of the daughter-in-law six months after the death of the mother-in-law.'

And troubles are sure to be imminent from confining within a narrow space a number of women

E

of different ages and of various forms of relationship,
who have little or nothing to do, and nothing
whatever to divert their minds from the most common-
place and trivial details. There may be two or more
wives of the same husband. Yet more probable is it
that there are aunts, sisters, sisters-in-law, daughters,
daughters-in-law, nieces, some married, some widows,
people of all ages and children of many degrees of
relationship. Friction in such families is inevitable.
Not only are there no means of escape from the
worry, annoyance, and tyranny that are but too
possible ; there is also no intellectual diversion of
mind or thought. What a refuge from trouble have
we in thoughts of the love, patience, and pity of God,
and in books ! They who love books have in them
an inexhaustible source of consolation and delight.
But a Hindu woman has neither. No one of the
numerous gods of whom she has any knowledge is
supposed to be loving, kind, and sympathetic.

And she has no books, nor could she read them
if she had. Of the 128,467,925 women in British
India in 1891, only 543,495 are returned as able to
read and write, with 197,662 learning. In the native
states female education is yet more backward, and if
it be remembered that at least one-third of the
readers are native Christians, it will be seen how few
have this advantage. Education, no doubt, is spreading, but more slowly than is supposed, and it is a new
thing ; for hundreds of years not one woman in two
thousand has been able to read or write—a well-

informed writer says 'one in 20,000'—and if they could have read previous to this half of the century, there was little for them to read that was not corrupting. This is proved by the second argument urged against female education—that women, notwithstanding all safeguards, are naturally predisposed to evil ; how much more so would they be if they read books ! The first being, that if women could read and write, they would be filled with the conceit that they were the equals of men.

Under such conditions of life ; assumed to be the inferiors of men, intellectually and morally ; to be unfit for freedom ; the subordinates of their husbands ; subject to the caprice and will of other women, related to them by marriage, not blood ; superstitious, ignorant, and without any elevating pursuits or associations, it is inevitable that they should be liable to untold sorrows and humiliations, and that even when they are not, their condition must be lacking in some of the most rational, benignant, and desirable elements of domestic life.

There are, however, some features of Hindu life and character which tend to alleviate and soothe the lot of women. They are much dwelt on by native apologists, and should in all fairness be stated.

Hindus are better than Hinduism, therefore their intelligence and humanity mitigate the tyranny and hardship of some of their customs. The women, for instance, feel their position to be less irksome than we suppose. Society from the top to the bottom has its foundation in despotism. As it rules unquestioned in the state, so does it in the family. Men rule and women submit as a matter of course ; unless the subjection can be evaded by favouritism or cajolery, and when the latter have never been taught that they have rights they can assert and claim, or seen or heard of anything but the most abject submission, and where the maxim is unquestioned, ' Whatever is, is best,' it is not so surprising that women acquiesce in their lot. They accept custom almost as patiently as they do a law of nature. Even when the knowledge comes to them that the condition of Western women is different from their own, it affects them far less than might be supposed, except as a thing to wonder at rather than to be sought for. ' They are a strange people ; they have one set of customs, we have another, and of course it is proper for each to follow its own,' expresses their thought, and there the matter ends ! Then, by a perverse method of reasoning and some caprice of fashion, that which to an Englishwoman would be intolerable, is regarded by her Hindu sisters as evidence of her husband's regard and of the respectability of her family. A woman who never walks abroad, and whose face is never seen but by women in the zenana, is as proud of being 'a purdah ' lady living behind a curtain as an Englishwoman whose husband keeps a carriage ; she regards it as a sign of rank, an evidence of her husband's care for her. Then the duties and amusements of such women, though trivial and unintellectual, are sufficient for them, since their minds are never opened to greater and more interesting affairs.

Nor is companionship always lacking. In such large and miscellaneous households, some can usually be found who in age, disposition, and sympathy become friends and helpers. And though the government of the family is despotic, giving a power too great and that may press heavily, even cruelly, on subordinates, it is not often so abused. Submission to authority is far more general than with us, and that disarms severity, and the gentleness and amiability of the Hindu character indisposes those who have power to abuse it, and those who have not power to provoke its. exercise.

Nor are husbands usually cruel or unkind. Brutality is not a Hindu characteristic. The husband may be indifferent, contemptuous, even unfaithful to his wife, but he is seldom cruel. Often he is indulgent in a patronizing way. He does not treat her as an equal, but his kindness, sense of honour, and affection induce him to please and humour her in ways he thinks suitable to her weak nature. She has the best food he can afford ; he loads her with ornaments, if not of gold and silver, of inferior material ; and not seldom she is the actual, though not the acknowledged ruler.

As large a proportion of Hindu women are gifted with great good sense, force of character, energy, grace of manner, charm, and beauty as will be found anywhere else, and these qualities exert their potency in India, as elsewhere. A Hindu gentleman, next to taking care that his caste is kept undefiled, regards it as his highest duty, his point of honour, to protect his female relatives. He thinks of them contemptuously and patronizingly, as weak, helpless, and liable to go astray, and his care degenerates into distrust and suspicion ; but in his own way, and according to his sense of propriety, he defends them from evil, pays them due respect, and ministers to their happiness in food, clothing, ornaments, and amusements, as far as his resources will allow ; and defends them from insult, dishonour, and danger as sternly as any knight of chivalry or modern gentleman. Indian history illustrates this in many romantic incidents.

Nevertheless, even when these modifying considerations are allowed their utmost weight, the normal condition of women leaves much to be desired. The masculine sentiment has ever been, ' Women are to be protected and cared for, not for their own sake, but because they are the potential or real mothers of men. They are necessary to us, and should for our repute be pleased and indulged as far as prudence will allow, according to their weak natures ; but since they are intellectually and morally weak, frivolous, vain, inclined to evil and to lead others astray, and unsteady as the lotus on the running stream, it is never safe to treat them as equals or to entrust them with power. Therefore they should not be left free, for their own sakes as well as ours. A woman is never fit for independence.'

The inevitable results of such sentiments, practically

acted on generation after generation, has been to make
men tyrants, women far less esteemed than they
should be, and their houses little better than prisons.
At the best, how colourless, dreary, degraded, and
unintellectual must be the lives of women who know
no more of nature than can be seen from their zenana
jilmills; who never walk abroad at their own free
will ; whose own husbands, fathers, brothers, treat
them, not as equals, not as companions, but as pretty
animals or pleasant toys ; whose opinions are never
consulted, and whose wishes are usually suspected ;
who have no inward sources of interest, information,
and delight from reading and writing ; and who never
are trusted without reserve. How ' cabined, cribbed,
confined,' are these millions, whose lives might be so
bright and fruitful of good and pleasantness !

But how seldom, alas ! is the highest ideal of any
state of society reached, and certainly it is seldom
reached in India. Reports, very reliable, speak of
extreme ignorance, jealousy, strife, petty tyranny,
unhappiness, much unhealthiness and disease, and
suicide as far from uncommon. And darker things
are said to be—illegitimacy, infanticide, murder.
The structure of society, the seclusion of Hindu
dwellings, and the jealous privacy of family life lend
themselves to the commission of such crimes, without
much fear of detection, and the glints of information which come to most who have opportunities of
learning what passes in private life justify these
statements. Testimony like the following is but too

abundant : 'The life of Hindu women is but a career of ignorance, servitude, and superstition.' 'We are prisoners,' says a Hindu lady, 'from our birth, and life-long sufferers ; and our fathers, brothers, husbands, sons, keep us in this prison. No Hindu brother pauses to think that it is to his own hurt to keep us down in this misery ; but it is. We women are shut up in a pit of ignorance. Hearing of our condition, the eyes of strangers fill with tears. But you leave us there. Have you no pity in your hearts ? '

Speaking of life in the zenana, another says, 'It is like that of a frog in a well : everywhere there is beauty, but we cannot see it ; it is hid from us.'

'Indian women,' says Mr. Dorabiji E. Gimi, 'are denied the common enjoyments of life, are throughout life behind purdahs, and, to add insult to injury, the excuse for all such unmanly conduct is proclaimed to be, their inborn wickedness.'

The following just and impartial statement is from a zenana missionary, in reply to the inquiry, 'Are Hindu women happy ? ' The latter part of it, however, takes account of some present-day conditions of life of which previous ages knew nothing.

'We all feel that they are remarkably apathetic under their sufferings. Apathy and a certain childishness are two leading features of their character, which may be accounted for partly by their long-continued state of subjection, and partly by their religion. They are taught to look at everything as ordered by fate, and they have been taught to regard themselves as inferior

to men in every way. Their minds are untrained and
easily diverted by trifles, and they have been brought
up to observe a multitude of small ceremonial par-
ticulars, and to regard these as essential. So it is no
wonder that they are dull and trifling, and that the
heavier sorrows of life seem sometimes hardly to
touch them—at least not acutely. It would be untrue
to say that they have not in a certain, dull, half-in-
articulate way, a feeling of their grievances. Some
express it, and others only show it in their careworn
and patient faces. But there cannot be much doubt
that the childish element in their character, the facility
with which they can be diverted from the consideration of their troubles by any little passing amusement,
goes a long way to lighten their burden. In the
better educated and more thoughtful, this facile disposition tends to disappear, and its place is sometimes
taken by a bitter sense of wrong and an inclination
to brood over grievances. And so in this case, as in
many cases of progress, there must be the inevitable
period of increased power to suffer without much increase in the relief of the suffering.

'Beside these natural characteristics there is an
external influence—the power of custom, perhaps
the strongest influence in a Hindu life. What is
customary is sacred, and rebellion against it hardly to
be thought of; and where rebellion is quite out of the
question, resignation of a kind follows, and produces
a measure of peace. But there are exceptions among
the classes, especially those which are least restricted.

'After saying so much about the dark side of things, it is only fair to say, too, that there are many really happy women among the Hindus and Mahomedans —happy, that is, in their outward circumstances and relationships. I am pretty certain that two-thirds of my present pupils have little or nothing to cause them suffering in the special ways common to the women of this country. They are kindly used, have the opportunity of learning, are not without outside interests, and seem on the whole to enjoy their lives. The things they lack, and which we most pity them for lacking, are things of the want of which they are not sensible.' [1]

[1] *The Mission World* for 1895, p. 421.

AN INDIAN WELL.

CHAPTER V.

CHILD LIFE.

NOWHERE is the sentence pronounced on Eve's daughters more manifestly carried out than in India. To the solicitudes of maternity, common to her sex, is added a load of anxiety as to the possible sex of her child ; for on that depends, for herself, an assured position if her child is a boy, dishonour if a girl. She is, at that time of mystery and tenderness, when she should have all possible sympathy, placed rather on trial, and kept in a state of extreme suspense ; for her future position and that of her child depends on that over which she can have no possible influence, but for which she may be blamed or praised, made happy or miserable.

She knows well that if she gives birth to a son, her family will be proud of her, her rivals and enemies—if she has any—humbled, and the fidelity, if not love, of her husband assured. And she knows, equally well, that the birth of a daughter will bring disappointment to her family, regret, and it may

be alienation, to her husband, and shame to herself.
It is not surprising, therefore, that the blessing
invoked on women over the greater part of India
should be, 'Mayest thou have eight sons, and may
thy husband survive thee ! '

Reference has been made to the supposed necessity
of having a son, for the well-being of the family in
a future life, and the stigma attached to being the
mother of daughters ; but it is important to observe
how and why such a mother is degraded.

In Hindu opinion, the conditions of this life arise
out of the merit or demerit contracted in a previous
state of existence, and, as women are held to be
inferior to men, to be born a woman is not only to
be born to an inferior position, but to give birth to
a girl is a sign of a lapsed, sinful taint in the soul,
which carries misfortune along with it.   To give
birth to a girl is held to be proof of evil inherited
and transmitted.   Men believe this, and women,
utterly ignorant and superstitious, who have never
had an opportunity to learn otherwise, cannot but
be strangely affected by such a belief.   How must
a wife thus placed yearn to give birth to a son, and
how must her heart sink within her, when, weak and
ill after the pangs of maternity, she is told, ' It is *only*
a girl' !   She may bewail her own misfortune in the
distinct fall of her status in the small circle in which
she lives, and if she can think, must pity the poor
little one, who is born to an inevitable inheritance
of humiliation.

Having these ideas of sex, its causes and consequences, it is not so surprising that the birth of a
daughter 'was followed by the quiet sign of the father's
depressed and slightly clenched thumb over the fingers
of the right hand. No word was needed, the old
nurse knew too well its signification, and as quietly
pressed her thumb on a well-known spot on the
child's head, and all was accomplished. Nor is it
surprising that many a mother, knowing the sad
probabilities of feminine life, sorrowfully acquiesced in
the deed as the less of two evils. And who can tell
how many such deeds of darkness still occur, even
daily, behind the purdah.'[1] If the poor little un-
welcome one is not destroyed by violence, she is sure
to be less cared for than a male child, possibly may
be neglected, and if disease or accident take her
away, her death will be accepted as a gain rather
than a loss.

Not only do the conditions of life suggest this, but
evidence confirms it. A lady medical missionary
writes : ' Often I say to myself with a choking feeling,
Alas! what has sin wrought ? Here is a poor
miserable child of three years, starved and ill. I order
cod-liver oil to be rubbed in her body, and the mother
says, " I don't think I'll take the trouble, for if she
dies I shall have one less to care for." ' Another lady
writes : ' In one of my houses I found a poor little
girl not more than three months old, lying wholly
neglected and uncared for, on the floor, crying very

[1] *Hindu Women*, by H. Lloyd, p. 38.

bitterly, and apparently in much pain, but no one came to render her any help. At last the grandmother appeared, but instead of taking her up, and comforting the little child, she showered anathemas upon the poor little thing, which greatly distressed me. So I asked the old woman to try and pacify the child ; but imagine my horror when she exclaimed, " Who cares for a girl ? If God could take away the boy, let him take the girl also. I am not going to touch her. I would rather she died." '

No doubt, far more generally, affection comes toward the little one, as well as pity, in the mother's heart, and in due time in the father's, for Hindu parents have this in no scant measure, overborne though it is by the all-powerful influence of popular opinion and superstition. But the affection is not directed by knowledge or intelligence. The father's love is mixed with contempt ; he recognizes her beauty, her pretty ways, her craving for pleasant food, for toys and amusements, and in these he indulges her—if he is good-natured and prosperous— to the utmost extent ; but her mind—well, he probably doubts if she has one, as he thinks he has, though he firmly believes in her innate weakness, frivolity, and inclination towards evil.

A girl is left almost entirely in the hands of her mother, and she, alas ! has no one qualification for such a task save that of affection. She is without knowledge, and with a mind entirely untrained and undisciplined, except by repression, suspicion, and coercion.

The chances are one to a thousand that she can neither read nor write. She has no knowledge to guide herself or to impart to her child ; for she has never mixed in society, nor had the opportunity to observe, nor talked to any one more intelligent than herself. But she is a devout worshipper of Siva, Krishna, Durga, and other terrible and licentious divinities. She holds some trees, animals, and stones to be sacred. She believes in omens, signs, lucky and unlucky persons, places, and occurrences, and in ghosts, evil spirits, and demons, and to her Eastern imagination they are real, terrible, and active. Perhaps she, a mother, is not far advanced in the teens. And other women in the family, if different in age, are equally ignorant, superstitious, and untrained. What must the daughter of such a mother become ? The child has more liberty than she ever will have in the future; she has at least the freedom of the house, and can play, with but little restraint, with her brothers and cousins. But she must keep within narrow bounds, she seldom sees a new face or hears a new voice, or is taken a mile from the place of her birth. Her toys and amusements are few and poor. She does not go to school ; she receives no intellectual training. All she is taught is how to stand and sit, to repeat a few prayers, that she may be protected from evil spirits, obtain a good husband who may live and will not take a second wife, and that her caste may not be defiled ! All the conversation she hears relates to cooking, doing *puja*, using terms of abuse, the legends

F

of a monstrous and licentious mythology, omens,
demons, and marriage. She has the two things a
child desires, but should not have, she is probably
indulged, and has no lessons to learn. But how dull
and uninteresting at the best such a life must be ;
without the laughter, sunshine, and flowers we always
love to associate with girlhood! And how ominous
of the future! And yet it is the happiest portion of
her life. She is freer than ever she will be in the
future. She dwells among her own people, where indulgence and affection prevail, and she is most likely
free from the worries and humiliations which invade
adult life.

But her time of happiness, restricted though it be
by the conditions of her sex and lack of education, is
very limited. There is not for her that exuberantly
sweet and glad time of maidenhood which makes the
lives of English girls, between the ages of twelve and
twenty-two, the happiest period of existence, and the
most free from care, of that enjoyed by human beings
of any age or country. Before that time comes, the
foolish, empty-minded women around her are specu-
lating about her marriage, and perhaps negotiating
for it ; and since festivals, legends, cooking, and matri-
mony are the four principal topics of their conversation, she is seldom left without more than sufficient
information of what is designed for her. Solicitude
as to her future, so largely dependent on a family of
strangers and so little on herself, comes to her at a
very early age, and abides with her whilst, after

marriage, she remains in her father's house, before being taken to that of her father-in-law.

This is not surmise: it is what we might expect from the conditions of our humanity and the state of society; and it is proved by the pathetic notices of which we so often read, of the sorrow and dread with which child-wives leave their own homes for those of their husbands, and then of their sorrowful yearning to be sent back again. And such untaught, untrained children have for many generations been the wives and mothers of the people!

HINDU ORPHANS.

CHAPTER VI.

CHILD MARRIAGE.

THE very early age at which marriage usually takes place needs to be proved, otherwise it would seem incredible. The great majority of girls are married before they are 12 years of age, an immense number before they are 10, and many even at an earlier age. The age varies with the caste and with the family, but it is exceedingly rare for any girl to be unmarried when 14 years of age, or any boy who is 16. Among the Brahmins marriage is earliest, and infants are often betrothed at the age of 2 or more years. Mr. Malabari gives the number of males in British India found married in 1881, up to 9, as 668,000, and the number of females 1,932,000. Between the ages of 10 and 14 the married males stood at 1,808,000, and married females 4,395,000. Between 15 and 19 the number of married males was 2,740,000, and of married females 5,323,000.

The census for 1891 gives the following returns of early marriages :—

Under 4 years of age, males ...	...	6945
,, ,, females	...	258.760
From 5 to 9 years, males ...	...	690,803
,, ,, females ...	...	2,201,404
From 10 to 14 years, males ...	...	2,342,433
,, ,, females	...	6,016,759

Sir W. W. Hunter says, 'In Bengal, out of every 1000 girls between 5 and 9 years of age, 271 are married. More than 10 boys in every 1000, between 5 and 10 years old, are bridegrooms; while of girls, 28 in 100 are wives or widows at an age when, if they were in Europe, they would be in the nursery or infant school. The Brahmins are 4'94 (rather less than 5) per cent. of the whole Indian population. The Brahmin female population in 1889 was 6,606,000; of this number 31 per cent. were widows, and 21⅔ per cent. unmarried.'

In England, out of every 100 females of 20 years of age and upwards, 25'80 are single, 60'60 are married and 13'60 widows. In the North-West Provinces

and Oude, the corresponding percentages are—
single, o·81 ; married, 69·64 ; widows, 29·55. ' From
5 to 11 is the usual period of marriage for Brahmin
girls all over India.'
The gravest evils, it can be shown,[1] are connected

[1] A specially repulsive form of polygamy and child marriage is
common in Bengal among Kulin Brahmins. It is a special honour to
be married to one of their rank, and they make a profession of it.
Instances are common of men who thus have married from ten to a
hundred wives without supporting any of them, and often never seeing
them after the marriage ceremonies and the receipt of the heavy
marriage dowry. The following instances quite sufficiently illustrate
the offensiveness of such a custom.

According to a correspondent of the Sangibani, a marriage was
recently performed between one of these much-married Brahmins and
fourteen girls belonging to one family. He writes: 'Sarbeshwar
Mukerji is a native of Belghoria, at present residing at Burdwan, aged
64 years. He is a Brahmin and a Kulin by birth, a polygamist by profession. The corresponding families, where he can marry by rules of
Debinor Ghatak, are the Banerjis of Amgram, in Fedipore district.
We learned that fourteen Misses Banarji were to be given away.
I went to the spot out of curiosity. I saw the bridegroom, older than
a grandfather, seated on a painted wooden seat, and fourteen girls,
varying in age from 3 to 26 years, seated before him in the form of a
crescent. The ladies were veiled, with faces cast down, as if cursing
their parents for shaming them.' This was not done a century ago.
It was done in the latter half of this year of grace 1897 (*Indian
Witness*).

'A Brahmin of Bengal gave away his 6 aunts, 8 sisters, and 4
daughters, in a batch of altogether 18, in marriage to one person—a boy
less than 10 years old. The brides of three generations were in age
from about 50 years to 3 months at the lowest. The baby bride was
brought to the ceremony on a brass plate. Among the Kulin Brahmins,
as a rule, the man who receives in marriage the majority of the
daughters of a family is bound to have the rest, otherwise the
minority must suffer a lifelong celibacy. Hundreds of instances like
the above may be given if needed ' (*Times of India*).

with this custom, and it has its absurd and ludicrous side. Such instances as the following are by no means rare. A young Brahmin in Calcutta, 16 years of age, was seen to be much depressed. On inquiry, he stated he was in trouble on account of his daughter's marriage. The class to which he belonged betroth their daughters immediately after birth. His trouble was that he could not find a suitable husband for his daughter, nor, if he could, had he the customary money to pay the usual heavy marriage expenses; hence the danger that his honour and respectability would be lowered !

We have heard of child bridegrooms, becoming frightened amid the din and excitement of marriage festivities, crying at the momentary absence of their mothers, and when somewhat quieted by the threat of a severe beating, sobbing, 'Where is my mother?'

Every missionary in charge of a good school is familiar with scenes like the following. A little fellow not in his teens, with the politeness inherent in his race, makes a request for leave of absence for three weeks, which always signifies that he is going to be married. 'But three weeks' absence will greatly interfere with your class work,' says the missionary. 'Yes, sir ; I am sorry, but I am obliged to ask leave.' 'Why?' 'I am going to be married, and all the arrangements have been made.' 'Have you ever seen the little lady you are to marry?' 'No, sir.'

The manner in which marriages are negotiated is twofold : either directly by the parents in mutual conference, or through the intervention of professional matchmakers, called *ghatuks*. Marriage is a delicate, difficult, and most expensive affair. Even some of the members of low-caste families are as punctilious in its arrangements as are Spanish grandees. Suitability of caste is the first and most vital consideration. Then the limits of consanguinity are carefully guarded. The husband must always be older than the wife, but, with strange inconsistency, whilst her seniority by one year would be a grave hindrance, *his* by twenty or even forty years would not usually be so considered. But higher conditions are not overlooked, for most parents are by no means indifferent to the social, moral, and physical qualities of those they bring into their families. Family life is far more isolated than with us. There is more suspicion and distrust, and none of that freedom which is one of the charms of English life ; for even if there be intercourse, it never becomes very confiding, or inclusive of the two sexes. Marriages, therefore, are never, as here, the result of intercourse, mutual inclination, and the gradual growth of affection on the part of those most concerned. Parents look out for suitable alliances among their neighbours and friends ; but since their opportunities for this and acquiring all necessary information are very limited, the services of the *ghatuks* are engaged— a useful class of women and men who make it their business to gather all the information possible of

eligible brides and bridegrooms, keeping, in fact, a
kind of registry office of all such cases for a whole
neighbourhood, for its convenience and their own
profit. When the most eligible person on the list
is selected, negotiations are commenced by the
ghatuk, and then by the fathers or some other
members of the families, until all the tedious and
intricate conditions as to time, ceremonies, and
expense are settled, or the negotiations broken off.
The actual marriage may be delayed for months, or
even years, and then usually a considerable period
elapses after marriage before the husband and wife
live together; he abides in his father's house, she in
her father's. But even in cases where they have lived
apart, never having seen each other but at a point
in the long and morally unedifying marriage rites,
she is doomed to a life of perpetual widowhood,
should her child husband die.

The origin and authority for early marriage are
worthy of inquiry. Like so many Hindu customs,
it claims a quasi-divine authority, and is based on
certain reasons which, from the Hindu point of view,
are of great weight. 'Reprehensible,' says Manu,
' is the father who gives not his daughter in marriage
at the proper time.' And all commentators say the
proper time is before the age of puberty. Thus
Gautama, 'A girl should be given in marriage before
she attains the age of puberty.' ' If,' says Vashista,
' a father neglects to give away his daughter after
a suitable age, he destroys himself.' A high legal

authority, Mr. Justice Moothoswami Tyer, recently said, 'According to custom now obtaining, a Brahmin girl is bound to marry, for fear of social degradation, before she attains maturity. Marriage is of the nature of a sacrament which no Brahmin is at liberty to neglect without forfeiting his caste.' He shows that the Smritis, or Things heard from God, 'declare it to be a duty of a father to bestow his daughter in marriage before she attains her maturity.' ' A father should try his best to perform the marriage of his daughter from the fourth year of her age upward, till before the completion of the tenth year'[1] (*Brahma Purana*). Thus a religious or sacramental purpose has been operative here, as in most other departments of Hindu life and thought. Marriage, as we have been assured repeatedly in recent native discussions, is a most sacred and important rite. Its leading idea is a belief in the necessity of offspring, not only that the funeral rites essential for the well-being of a father's soul may be duly performed, but that the ritual and service necessary for the family ancestors may be perpetuated by competent descendants. As Mr. Barnes, the Census Commissioner for Bombay, says, 'According to the ideal code of Manu, every man ought to marry, in order that he may have a son to perform at his death the sacrifices to his

---

[1] 'For girls 9 and 10 are middling good ages for marriage, 11 a bad age, and 12 is one requiring the observance of penance to wipe away the sin. If a girl resides under the roof of her father unmarried up to 12 years of age, her father commits a sin ' (*Dharma Sindhu*, a modern work on Hindu law).

ancestors, and pour out the customary libation to their spirits. Without such ceremonies the father's soul cannot be delivered from the hell called "Putt." As regards the father of a damsel, it is his duty to see her married, as she is put into the world to become a mother.'

There follows from this exaggerated idea of the necessity for male offspring, a corresponding want of mindfulness for the happiness of parents. It has been said, 'In the elaborate Hindu marriage ritual, the happiness of the married couple is not mentioned, either as a primary or secondary purpose of marriage. Its main ingredient is a desire for offspring as a necessity of religion.'

Among the inducements to child-marriage are those which proceed from the superstition, ignorance, and love of excitement on the part of mothers and other feminine members of the family. They, much more than the other sex, press forward all initial arrange-ments for marriage, and are restless until the long, elaborate, expensive, and by no means refined rites are completed. And the two general characteristics of Hindu women explain why it is so. To have a daughter well and early married is the fixed idea of the mother. She talks to her child continually of this, almost from its infancy. Poor woman! there is little beside that she can talk about. She cannot read or write ; she seldom hears others read, and if she does, it is most likely from books tedious in their speculativeness, or wild and indecent in their narratives of gods, demons, or men. She has probably never even listened once to an intelligent conversation. What does she know, and what can she teach?

HINDU WATER-CARRIER.

Her ideas are necessarily few, intense, and concentrated on what is around her. But she is superstitious, affectionate, and a slave to custom. To her foolish mind it never occurs that her daughter may remain unmarried until womanhood, or never marry at all. That would seem to her unnatural and disgraceful, since in her inane, most uninteresting life, a birth, a death, a great religious festival, and a marriage are almost the only events which break its dreariness. She is much more disposed, both from a mistaken sense of duty and a craze for pleasure, to hasten on than to retard the event.

Some of the causes originating and perpetuating this pernicious custom may be further indicated. The gloomy distrust and suspiciousness of Indo-Aryan human nature has been one of these. This characterizes most Eastern races, but Hindus more than any other. It prevails not only toward strangers, and those vested with power, but enters into the more intimate relations of common life. How far this is inherent as a race quality, and how far the product of a weird and gloomy superstition and of centuries of oppression, wrong, and untruthfulness, cannot now be considered. The fact remains that this is a marked feature of character exhibited toward men, demons, and even gods, but concentrated with a force often malignant and contemptuous on all womankind. From the dreadful text of Manu, already given in the first chapter, it is clear that these sentiments were prevalent some two thousand years ago. The construction of Hindu family life, in all its customs and details, reflects this low opinion of woman's power to take care of herself. One purpose, therefore, of wedlock is to guard her from her own self, as well as from outward peril. The sentiment and the custom to which it has led is a long-standing insult of two thousand years' duration against all womankind.

There has been one strong incentive to early marriage, which in the past might be urged in its justification. The unsettled, precarious conditions of life, from the remotest times until the establishment of British power, encouraged parents to have their children married as soon as possible, as a means of defence and safety. Their lives were usually exposed to peril and death. Even whilst the parents lived, their power to protect their children from evils worse than death was often inadequate. And when Mahomedanism became dominant, a new danger threatened daughters, through the sensual and polygamous proclivities always characteristic of that creed. Parents, therefore, in former ages distrustful of their children and of all men, and of their own ability to insure the safety of the weakest portion of their families, have been eager to secure protectors for them by early marriage.

One original motive for early marriage, as powerful as any other, and perhaps the origin of the custom, was that Hindu female virtue should by all means be secured. The sentiment was alike honourable to the affections, morals, and high sense of the value of family integrity prevalent in early times, and of great power to-day. But the ancient Aryans were probably unconscious of the sinister aspect of their policy, and certainly did not foresee the abuses and evils to which it would lead ; for whilst it tells ol times of rapine and violence, prevalent throughout all the ages of Indian history prior to our own, and of parental affection and care, it has come to indicate an entire lack of confidence in the honour and virtue of Hindu men, and a base, unworthy idea of Hindu women.

CHAPTER VII.

INFANTICIDE.

INFANTICIDE has been common in India from the remotest times ; but native writers give us no information of a reliable kind on this or any of the main features of social life, so that our knowledge, at the best imperfect, is confined to the present century, the period of British supremacy.

Three causes have led to it—

1. Great moral laxity, combined with indifference to infantine life, and a desire to conceal wrong-doing, which the privacy of native habits renders comparatively easy.

2. Religious fanaticism has led to the crime in restricted areas.

Among the Khonds of Orissa and the Central Provinces, children were stolen or purchased by groups of villages, that, being sacrificed to the earth goddess, their blood might secure a plentiful harvest on all the fields on which it was shed.[1]

The offering of children to Gungama, by casting

[1] See Numbers XIV. and XV. of *Calcutta Review*.

them into the sacred stream, especially at Allahabad, where the Jumna and Ganges meet, and at Gunga Saugor, where the great river enters the sea, were common in former times. Such places being regarded as specially sacred, and therefore conferring on the act additional merit.

3. But infanticide, springing out of disappointment at the birth of girls, because of their assumed inferiority to boys, the lowering of the family repute, and the inevitable expense demanded by usage on their marriage, chiefly requires our attention ; because it grew into a system which was hardly concealed, and became prevalent in Rajputana, Gujarat, Cutch, and other great districts in Central and Western India, inhabited by proud, brave, well-to-do races, who therefore were free from the temptations to the crime from poverty, want, and the dread of suffering, so often leading to its commission in other countries. And its marked peculiarity everywhere in India is that, unless to avoid disgrace and punishment, girls, not boys, are destroyed.

It is advisable to give a number of well-authenti-cated statements, from undoubted authorities on this subject, for the reason alleged by Lord Teignmouth, as far back as the close of last century, when he and others first became aware of the systematic nature of the atrocity—'That the practice of infanticide should ever be so general as to become a custom, with any sect or race of people, requires the most unexceptionable evidence to gain belief.' And the evidence is alike unexceptionable, varied, and abundant.

A Resident of Benares, after a circuit through the country inhabited by the Rajkumars, records, that in conversation with several persons, 'all unequivocally admitted that infanticide was customary.'

In 1800, when officiating Governor of Bombay, Mr. Duncan stated, on the authority of the Newab of Surat, that among the Rajputs, 'the birth of a daughter was considered disgraceful,' and many were put to death.

Many such reports led Mr. Duncan to institute careful inquiries, which brought to light such startling facts as the following: 'Among the Jharija inhabitants of Cutch, the far greater part followed the practice without remorse.' So was it 'throughout the province of Gujarat.' 'The lowest estimate was, that in Kattiawar about 1000, and in Cutch 2000 were annually destroyed.' It was found that the custom was prevalent among the Rajputs of Jeipore and Jhoudpore, the Jhats, and Mewats, 'and other tribes of Hindustan.' 'Indeed, we may assume it'—reports Colonel Walker, who conducted the investigations—'as an unquestionable fact, that the existence of female infanticide prevails to a far greater extent in India than has yet come under the observation of the British Government.'[1]

This general statement was based on a large number of facts, of which the following are specimens :—

[1] *Calcutta Review*, August, 1844, and *Parliamentary Papers*, 1824-28.

'A register of a district in Kattiawar was made by the Bombay Government in 1817, and the whole number of female children in 81 towns and villages was only 63.' 'In 157 Kichi Rajput families, there were found by an English official, only 32 daughters, while there were 189 sons.' 'In another group of 63 families there were 19 daughters, but 75 sons.'

'Elsewhere among other people and in another province, in 13 villages, among 654 families, he found more than 429 boys under 12 years of age, but only 110 girls, some of the people admitting that every girl born in their villages had been destroyed.'

Coming down a few years later, we find similar statements. Thus:

'In a few villages in the Rajput state of Udiapore, containing about 500 families, there were at least 350 boys, while there were not above 90 girls; and in four villages in another adjoining state, containing 144 families, there were found to be above 90 boys under 12 years of age, and only 10 girls; while in one village, where there were 22 boys, the inhabitants confessed that they had destroyed every girl born there.' [1]

Mr. Wilkinson, a political agent in Rajputana, said in an official paper dated 1836, 'An intelligent Rajput chief, in conversing with me, stated as his opinion that not less than 20,000 infants were annually destroyed in the whole of Malwa and Rajputana.' There is now before me an elaborate table, taken from the first volume of the Royal Asiatic Society's

[1] *Calcutta Christian Observer* for 1834, pp. 183, 471.

Transactions of a Rajput population in Cutch of about
4000, living in 114 towns and villages, among which
there were 815 boys, but only 144 girls.

' By the spontaneous admission of the guilty parties
themselves, it was ascertained that in one tribe the
proportion of sons to daughters was 118 to 16; in a
second, 240 to 98; in a third, 131 to 61; in a fourth,
14 to 4; in a fifth, 39 to 7; in a sixth, 20 to 7; and
in a seventh, 70 to 32.'

This was among Rajputs, but the usage was by
no means confined to them. Of eleven villages of
Puriar Minas, Mr. Wilkinson, a political agent, ascertained, from a carefully conducted inquiry, ' that the
aggregate number of boys under 12 years of age was
369, and of girls only 87.' ' In one village there
were only 4 girls, but 44 boys; in another, 4 girls to
68 boys; and in a third, with a large proportion of
boys, no girls at all, the inhabitants freely confessing
they had destroyed every girl born in the village.' [1]

Such statements as these were corroborated by
almost all who paid attention to the subject, and

---

[1] The British officer before alluded to, who, in Western India,
endeavoured to suppress the practice, tells the following startling
incident : '.As I was riding out one morning, I passed through the
Bunde Mina village of Muur. I was there beset by the cries of a
Mina woman, the wife of one of the watchmen, who clamorously
demanded of me to forbear all endeavours to procure the suppression
of an ancient custom and a religious rite, enjoined on them by divine
authority. When I endeavoured to pacify the unfeeling woman, she
boldly averred that daughters of their tribe had been foretold, if
preserved, to bring only trouble and misfortune to their families, and
that the event could not but be calamitous.'

were in a position to obtain the most reliable information. Thus Sir Henry Pottinger writes, 'I quite concur with Mr. Wilkinson, that infanticide is carried on to an extent of which we have hardly yet a complete notion in India.' One official reports that 'it prevailed among the Rajput tribes in the vicinity of Gwalior;' another that 'it was not uncommon among the Rajputs of the Jabalpore district;' another, that 'it abounded in the territory of the Rajah of Rewah;' another, that 'in Scindia's territory the usage does not appear to be restricted to any individual class or particular rank of life—that Gugurs and Jats, with the Rajputs, rich and poor, high and low, must be reckoned as different classes of people who put to death all the female infants born in their families; that exceptions from this general principle are rare, and that in the district of Sekarwari alone from two to five hundred were commonly put to death every year.'[1]

Think of such a custom prevalent for generations, over states and districts large and populous as Portugal, Ireland, and Switzerland, and what an aggregate of crime, shame, and suffering it suggests!

A painful interest attaches to the methods by which these little ones were slain. These differed in various districts and nationalities. In some they killed their infant daughters, or allowed them to die, by denying them all sustenance from their birth. In others the infant was often strangled. They were poisoned by

[1] *Calcutta Review*, 1844, p. 384.

the juice of the madder plant, or of the tobacco leaf,
or the datura plant, or the juice of the poppy, often

HINDU INFANTICIDE.

placed on the mother's breast. They were drowned
in pans of milk; suspended in baskets on trees;

buried alive in shallow graves ; left out at night
to be devoured by jackals ; or, if near the sacred
Ganges, thrown in, with an invocation to the goddess
to be pleased to accept the gift. So deep rooted and
established was the practice, that the child was often
put to death without so much as apprising the father
of its existence. If he was informed, the brief reply,
'To do as is customary,' or the half-indignant, half-
contemptuous remark, 'It is nothing,' or a gesture,
or total silence, was well understood, and acted on
without expostulation or further remark.

The little ones were usually destroyed immediately
after birth. Some features of the dreadful custom
require special attention.

Infanticide in India has usually sprung from causes
such as have not led to the crime elsewhere. Poverty,
the difficulty of rearing children in troubled times or
sterile regions, heartless indifference and want of
natural affection, have been its principal causes in
other countries. In India, where none of these causes
have been permanently and powerfully active, it yet
became an established custom, more systematically
practised by the upper than the lower castes and
classes, and confined as a custom to one sex.

The reasons for such a usage, widely established
among such people, and perpetuated through many
generations, are worthy of close attention.

Cruelty is not a Hindu characteristic. It has never
been reduced to a system, as by North American
Indians, or Chinese. But the people are callous

and apathetic. They would not deliberately inflict suffering and take pleasure in it, but they would not move hand or foot to rescue such as were greatly suffering. They do not suffer by knowing that others suffer. Therefore suffering and sorrow and wrong never evoke private or public indignation and protest. This goes far to explain the unchallenged prevalence for ages of such atrocities as suttee and infanticide.

Then, human life is not valued and held sacred, as with us. The great prevalence of all forms of life ; the intensity of a gloomy imaginativeness, on fixed pantheistic, fatalistic, and metempsychosis conceptions, leading to the idea that all life partakes of the same material, evanescent, gross qualities, which if suppressed in one form will appear in another, lowers their idea of the value and sacredness of human life. That great conception of man as superior to all other living creatures because possessed of a soul, which adds so much to the sacredness and dignity of human life in our eyes, Hinduism knows nothing of ; life, therefore, is not reverenced as it is with us, unless its distinct use is apparent.

And there is such a use supposed to belong to male, but not to female life. A son is essential to a family, a daughter is not, but is rather regarded as a failure, an encumbrance, and a dishonour.[1]

---

[1] 'Though one may have attained the dignity of a prince, if he be without male offspring, he liveth not' (*Bramhotura Candam*).

'Not by the power of charitable acts, not by fasting, not by burnt offerings, can mortals obtain salvation ; unless male offspring be obtained, there is no happiness either in this world or in the next' (*Baradam*).

'A mother of sons' is one of the highest compliments that can be paid to a wife; 'a mother of daughters' is one of the most contemptuous and scornful of all terms of reproach. This explains the gladness with which the birth of sons is welcomed, the disappointment manifest at the birth of daughters, and the disposition to put them away. 'When a female is born, no anxious inquiries await the mother; no greetings welcome the new-comer, who appears an intruder on the scene, which often closes in the hour of its birth.' 'It is nothing,' indicates the feminine sex of the little one, or with equal contempt and more explicitness, 'It is only a girl.'

When death was determined on, it usually followed immediately after birth, for it was considered barbarous to deprive a child of life after it had lived a day or two.

And infanticide is, perhaps, the most easily perpetrated of all crimes, and the most easy to conceal, when concealment is desired. The frailty of child life, the strict privacy of zenanas, the reticence of the people, and their indifference to feminine child life, all tended to favour a practice which was regarded more generally as the evasion of a misfortune than the commission of a crime. 'For what is easier to destroy than the blossom of a flower?'

But whilst these were the causes generally operative, there were two special ones, which were influential among the haughty, high-caste Rajputs and kindred tribes—the difficulty of procuring suitable husbands for their daughters, when the customary

age for marriage arrived ; with the supposed disgrace
of having unmarried daughters, and the difficulty of
defraying the heavy expenses which usage demands.
No families in the world, not even those of the
reigning houses of Europe, are more punctilious on
all questions of marriage and lineage. The conditions and limitations of a suitable alliance are
extraordinarily minute, yet so binding, that the
Rajput would rather kill his child, and indeed in
many cases himself, than endure what he considers,
both to his race and caste, an indelible disgrace.[1]
The excessive amount of marriage expenses has
been a fruitful cause of infanticide, and the pressure
toward ostentation and excess is felt more by the
higher castes and classes than the lower ; and
nowhere more than among the Rajputs. Into
details of the various items of expenditure, it is
unnecessary to enter ; it is sufficient to say that what
with gifts to the tribe, to Brahmins, minstrels, beggars,
and profuse festivities for days and even weeks, the
expenditure often amounted to one-half or more of
the year's income, or an equivalent amount, borrowed
at 20 or 40 per cent. interest, and entailing a heavy
burden of debt on the family for years. Many
instances are on record of from 2000 to 5000 guests
being entertained on such occasions, many of them
expecting and receiving a gift ; of gifts to favoured

---

[1] A confidential agent of the Rajah of Cutch admitted that daughters
were not reared in his master's family, and being asked why, replied,
' Where have they an equal on whom to be bestowed in marriage ? '

priests and minstrels of hundreds and even thousands of pounds; of the total expenses of a marriage amounting to ten thousand pounds, and of families reduced from opulence to poverty by this senseless yet exacting custom.

There was a close and subtle connection between infanticide and suttee, a rite common in Rajput families of distinction. The latter suggested and encouraged the former. Suttee (literally the 'method of purity') was sanctioned by the Shastras, extolled as a most meritorious act by the Brahmins, and not unfrequently encouraged by male relatives as a meritorious and convenient method for disposing of female relatives who had become an encumbrance, and were regarded as a dishonour. 'If,' reasoned the Rajput father, 'we encourage a widow to die thus for our convenience, her merit, and to preserve her honour, surely we may destroy an infant daughter, by starvation, suffocation, or neglect, of whose marriage in the line of caste and family dignity there is so little prospect;' and the Rajput mother, knowing what the life of a woman might be, and how it might terminate, would be inclined sorrowfully to acquiesce in the decision. When a woman was expostulated with for putting her children to death, she replied, 'Would that my mother had killed me, for what a miserable lot is mine, serving a cruel and tyrannical husband!'

The English Government, in harmony with the humane and benevolent policy for which it has ever been distinguished, has discouraged and forbidden

infanticide. But its power to repress the crime has
not been equal to its will. Three causes especially
have stood in its way—the difficulty of suppressing an
immemorial family usage ; the ease and secrecy with
which the usage may be carried out ; and especially
the fact that our power to make laws affecting the
social life of the people was limited to a comparatively
small area of India during the earlier decades of the
century, and that even now we have no such absolute
power in the states where infanticide has been for
ages most prevalent. In the latter instances the
moral influence of the British Government has been
repeatedly exerted against the practice, and not in
vain. But wherever its power is supreme, infanticide
has been made a penal offence.

It is unnecessary to do more than state that as
long ago as 1802 the Government enacted laws for
the suppression of infanticide; that subsequently, as
the British dominions extended, the prohibition was
declared and enforced ; and that, as the practice was
ascertained to be common as recently as 1870, the
Legislative Council passed the Female Infanticide
Act, which gave power to all magistrates to use
special means for the suppression of the crime
wherever it was supposed to be prevalent. This has
checked, though it has not eradicated, the evil, as
the following reports show : In the Administration
Report of the North-West Provinces for 1881-82, the
number of proclaimed villages was 2368. In the
report for 1883-84 it is stated that the crime was

greatly lessened. In 1886–87 the practice is reported
as yet further diminished, and the proclaimed villages
to be reduced to 1573 ; and in 1887–88, to 1381.

Mr. Unwin, magistrate, Mynpoure, in the North-
West Provinces, observing the absence of female
children in villages inhabited by Chohan Rajputs,
instituted a system of inspection to check infanticide.
All village watchmen were called on to report the
births of female children to the police, who reported
the cases to the magistrate. A month afterwards
the health of the child was to be reported on. If it
died under suspicious circumstances, a post-mortem
examination had to be held. In six years after the
institution of this inspection there were 1263 girls in
the Chohan villages of the Mynpoure district, whilst at
the beginning of the six years there were none at all !

Happily, the crime is abating through the persistent
action of the Government, and yet more because of
that great wave of renewed opinion and sentiment
passing over the people.[1] But that this crime is yet

---

[1] One of the most auspicious indications of this change was in 1888,
when forty delegates, many of them of high rank, and deputed to
represent various Rajput states, met to consider how the abuses connected with female marriage could be corrected. Several days were
spent in conference, and resolutions of a definite nature were passed,
recommending many important reforms.

Referring to the age of marriage, the delegates reported, 'As a rule,
boys and girls are married at an early age, notwithstanding that the
evils of such a custom are well known to all, and need no description.
It seems proper that boys and girls should not marry before the age of
18 and 14 respectively.' The following recommendations, intended to
limit marriage expenses, suggests the wasteful extravagance commonly
practised. 'On the marriage, for instance, of the Thakur, or his son

frequent, and the law evaded, is evident from four facts :—

1. The Census returns for 1880-81 showed that in all India there were fewer women than men by over five millions.

In 1891 the men were 146,727,000 ; the women, 140,496,000.

2. The Census returns for 1870 revealed that in one year 300 children were carried off by wolves and jackals from the city of Umritsur, and they all happened to be girls !

3. Even in 1894 the following confirmatory evidence has been given. At the sitting of the Opium Commission in January, Miss Greenfield, superintendent of a mission hospital for women at Ludiana, said, ' Fathers insisted on daughters being killed, to avoid the expense of weddings.' At the sitting of the Commission at Umballa, Miss Carter, a medical missionary, said, ' She knew one mother who had destroyed seven children. Women could easily do this by opium.'

4. Vice is prevalent in all Indian society, and is almost shameless ; but an illegitimate child is rarely seen.

or daughter, if the value of the estate was above R. 20,000, not more than one-fourth of the annual income was to be spent. When the income was below R. 10,000, but above R. 1000, not more than one-half was to be spent.'

Referring to the conference and its decisions, Lord Cross stated in the House of Lords that ' it was the greatest advance—in Indian social reform—made in the present century, and might lead to changes which no man living could foresee.'

CHAPTER VIII.

HAPPILY suttee has long ceased. By a decree of the Indian Government, dated December 4, 1829, it was declared illegal by the criminal courts. Not only was the intended suttee to be restrained and punishable, but all persons convicted of aiding and abetting in the sacrifice of a widow, by burning or burying alive, were deemed guilty of culpable homicide, and liable to punishment by fine, by imprisonment, or by both. This was followed the year after by similar decrees by the Madras and Bombay Governments. No resistance, and but the feeblest protest was raised against the prohibition, and but in the rarest instances, even in the independent states, has this atrocity ever since been perpetrated.

Why, then, devote even a brief chapter to an obsolete custom, viewed by all intelligent Hindus of our age with regret and shame? Because it was practised more or less for long centuries; was regarded as a most exemplary and meritorious deed; had its *raison d'être* in Hindu sentiment; and was one of the most singular and repellent customs that any intelligent and mild-mannered race ever practised.

Let it not be assumed that the practice was universal, or even general. It was almost restricted to the higher classes and castes, and to certain portions of the vast peninsula. It was most customary in the great province of Bengal, and especially in the districts around Calcutta. But in the North-West Provinces, in Rajputana, Gujarat, Malwa, and Orissa, suttees were frequent.

The custom was prevalent in Java, where once the Hindus had power, and one low caste in North-East India, the Jogees—weavers—encouraged the burying alive of widows.

It is impossible to say to what extent this rite was prevalent in times prior to British rule.[1]

Statistical information is the indirect outcome of

[1] From the following extract it is clear that suttee must have been common, at least on the eastern coast of India, 300 years ago : ' They had a custom that if any Hindu died, the wife had to burn herself of her own free will ; and when she was proceeding to this self-sacrifice it was with great merry-making and blowing of music, saying that she desired to accompany her husband to the other world. But the wife who would not so burn herself was thrust out from among the others, and lived by gaining, by means of her body, support for the maintenance of the pagoda of which she was a votary. However, when Affonso de Albuquerque took the city of Goa, he forbade, from that time forward, that any more women should be burned ; and although to change one's customs is equal to death itself, nevertheless they were happy to save their lives, and spoke very kindly of him because he had ordered that there should be no more burning.'—Albuquerque's *Commentaries*, vol. ii. p. 94.

Christian civilization, and where the latter is not influential, the former is vague and unreliable. Then, too, an instinct of our humanity disposes races even far less advanced than Hindus to conceal, or at least to be reticent about, their deeds of darkness. Therefore, African tribes are silent about cannibalism, the Chinese on infanticide, and some negro and Hindu sectaries relative to their secret forms of worship. All through the East it is easy, and apparently ever has been, to hide crime. Two features, however, of this strange custom we do know—that it was practised long ages ago, and that it was of very common occurrence, especially in Bengal and North-Western India, at the beginning of this century.

Two ancient European writers, Diodorus Siculus and Strabo, before the Christian era, notice it as one of the peculiar customs of the East, which greatly interested and perplexed all the Greeks who had any knowledge of Indian life. Thus we may infer that for two thousand years at least this Moloch devoured annually a proportion of hapless Hindu widows.

But at the beginning of this century we come to proximate data. It could not be otherwise that, when the British were well established in Bengal, where suttees were most common, their attention should be drawn to a custom so repellent to all their own usages.

The earliest movement in this direction was made by the Serampore missionaries. In 1801, Dr. Carey wrote, ' I consider that the burning of women, the burying of them alive with their husbands, the exposure of infants, and the sacrifice of children at Saugor, ought not to be permitted, whatever religious motives are pretended, because they are crimes against the state.'

In 1804, the missionaries sent ten agents to travel from village to village within a circle of thirty miles from Calcutta, to collect information, when it was found that more than 300 widows had been immolated on the funeral pile within six months!

Subsequent inquiry showed that in twelve years, from 1815 to 1826, 7154 widows thus perished in the Presidency of Bengal, more than half of them taking place in the Calcutta division. In one year the number rose to 839.

In eight of the years between 1815 and 1826 there were 287 such combined murders and suicides in the Madras Presidency, and in that of Bombay 284 in nine years. There are adequate reasons for supposing that these figures are below the number actually immolated; yet more certain is it that they do not express the full extent of the evil. They include no information relative to the vast populations of Oude, the Punjab and Rajputana, in each of which the rite was certainly more frequent than in South India.

It is unnecessary to attempt any description of the horrors that in every instance must have been associated with the rite, but two features of frequent occurrence serve to heighten its general repulsiveness.

One was the tender age of many of these victims ; the other, the number of widows sometimes thus destroyed at the same time.

A list is given in the Parliamentary papers on Suttee, vol. v. p. 17, of sixty-one widows all under 18 years of age, who thus perished between 1815 and 1820.

Age ...	17	16½	16	15	14	13	12	10	8
Number	14	1	22	6	2	2	10	1	3

In the Calcutta division there were, in 1826, 279 suttees—more than five every week ; and of these seventy-eight were under 40 years of age. In the *Asiatic Journal* for Sept., 1827, occurs the remark, ' It is lamentable to find that of the 24 young creatures under 20 years of age who underwent the cruel rite in 1824, one was aged 13, another 11, and another only 9.'

In many instances several wives were immolated. At the close of last century, a Kulin Brahmin died three miles from Serampore. He had married more than forty wives, of whom twenty-two died before him. At his obsequies a great fire was prepared, into which all the remaining eighteen threw themselves, leaving more than forty children. In another instance, about the same time, twenty-two women thus died at Nuddea in Bengal. This Brahmin polygamist had more than 100 wives. The fire was burning for three days, and as the wives arrived they were immolated, for only three lived with him ; the rest he had seldom

seen. He had married four sisters in one house.
Some of those who thus perished were 40 years of
age, others were as young as 16. In one instance
given in a Government report for 1812, a Brahmin
had married twenty-five wives. Thirteen had died in
his lifetime, but the remaining twelve all perished on
his funeral pile, leaving thirty children. Such instances
were not common, since polygamy is not frequent,
excepting with Kulin Brahmins; but instances of the
juvenility of widows thus sacrificed, and of other
suttee widows being the mothers of two, three, or
more children, were of very frequent occurrence.

How came a custom so terrible and revolting to be
so widely and permanently recognized? Several
causes, physical, social, and religious, contributed to it.
These had relation more or less to the widows themselves, their husbands, their families, the priesthood,
and society generally.

Diodorus Siculus explained that the rite was
encouraged, if not enforced, as a check on the
poisoning of husbands by their wives.

' This wicked practice increasing, and many falling
victims to it, and the punishment of the guilty not
serving to deter others from the commission of the
crime, a law was passed that wives should be burned
with their deceased husbands, except such as were
pregnant and had children, and that any individual
who refused to comply with this law should be
compelled to remain a widow, and be for ever excluded
from all rights and privileges, as guilty of impiety.

This measure being adopted, it followed that the abominable disposition to which the wives were addicted was converted into an opposite feeling. For, in order to avoid that climax of disgrace, every wife, being obliged to die, not only took all possible care of their husband's safety, but emulated each other in promoting his glory and renown. Strabo is of the same opinion.'[1]

This may not be an adequate explanation, but it is not entirely to be set aside, remembering that universal distrust and suspicion, especially of women, seems formerly, as now, to have been general; and certainly it has been one of the fostering causes of perpetual widowhood, an incentive for wives to take the utmost care of their husbands, since, however base and unworthy they might be, their state was better with them than without them—they could not have others.

A woman, according to Hindu sentiment, is not an entity by herself, as a man is. There is no equality whatever between them. He was created to rule, she to serve. So entirely is she subordinate, that she has no place in life but to serve his purposes and pleasure. Therefore she begins to fulfil her vocation in life when he marries her, and her vocation in life is ended when he dies. Henceforth she has no true or useful place in life. She is as a flower plucked, as a weed even, only to be cast aside. She is a

---

[1] *India's Cries to British Humanity*, p. 127, by James Peggs; *Asiatic Journal* for 1823 and 1827.

burden on her husband's family, and a dishonour.
For all such there was no future, no hope. Life had
lost for them that one only feature which made it
desirable in the estimation of the small circle in
which each widow lived, but which to them was all
the world. To them the sweetness and the light had
passed out of life ; there was, therefore, so much less
to live for. And the personal as well as relative
inducements to flee from the ills they too well knew,
were very great. Death and torture are less terrible
to those of pure Asiatic race than to us. They are
sensitive, kind, pitiful, and can meet and even dare
death, whether by disease or violence, with a calmness
unusual with Europeans. Then the widow's honour
or vanity was appealed to. The suttee was praised
and held in repute as the most faithful and estimable
of wives by priests and sages. For instance, Ungera
recommends the usage thus : 'The woman that
mounts the funeral pile of her deceased husband
enjoys bliss in heaven with him for three and a half
crore (35 million years), and with her own power
taking her husband up in the same manner as a snake-
catcher takes a snake out of its hole ; if he be bound
in hell with strong chains, yet she takes him by the
hand and leads him to heaven by the force of her
piety.' 'She that goes with her husband to the other
world purifies three generations, that is, the generations of her mother's side, father's side, and husband's
side ; and so she, being reckoned the purest and best
in fame among women, becomes dear to her husband,

and continues to please herself with him for a period equal to the reign of fourteen Indras ; and although the husband be guilty of the sin of slaying a Brahmin or friend, or be ungrateful of past deeds, yet she is capable of purifying him from all these sins.'

Haruta adds a very significant inducement to these. ' After the death of a husband, until his wife does burn herself in the fire, she cannot get rid of her feminine body.' And, finally, the Mahabharat says, that a widow, thus dying, atones by such a meritorious deed for being a shrew or even unfaithful all through her married life, and secures her husband's company in a future state, even if he is indifferent to her, or she become a suttee through wrath, fear, or unlawful affection.

It is not so surprising, therefore, that a proportion of women, quite ignorant, very devout, affectionate, vain, and with really little or nothing to make life dear to them, should have accepted this method of leaving the world, which to them would be but too literally a vale of tears, for one which to their superstitious fancy was to be a sure paradise for at least millenniums of years.

The number of widows often found in families where the resources of the family are very limited is now a ground of complaint. She is a reproach to a house as well as a burden. She usually lives with her husband's family, not her own, and her presence, therefore, is the less tolerable. Her existence militates against favourable terms in negotiating the marriages

of other girls in the family. It was an honour to a
family for its widows to become suttees, an honour
with their neighbours, a merit with the gods. What
wonder, then, that women were encouraged thus to die ;
nay, that not seldom, as credible testimony declares,
they were often threatened, constrained, and drugged
for the purpose ?

But the sanction given to suttee by religion was the
great cause of its practice and perpetuation. As we
have seen, it was regarded as a most holy and meritorious deed, the most appropriate method in which
a true wife could end her life, and having such merit
and efficacy that, even in spite of obstacles, it carried
the suttee to beatification for millions of years, and
brought to her family untold blessings. The sages,
always regarded by Hindus as more or less divine
and inspired, taught all this ; the people, ever disposed
to look at all things in a religious light, implicitly
accepted these ideas, and the Brahmins encouraged
and fostered them. They were the directors on all
such occasions, officiating by virtue of their sacred
character, encouraging the victim, not seldom constraining her, and gaining for themselves no small
amount of merit and reputation. They were the
prominent actors in almost every instance of suttee of
which we have a record. And they encouraged the
opinion that the rite was meritorious and sacred. As
Colebroke says, ' The bystanders throw on butter and
wood ; for this they are taught that they acquire merit
exceeding ten millionfold the merit of an *aswamedha*

or other great sacrifice. Even those who join the
procession from the house of the deceased to the
funeral pile, for every step are rewarded as for an
aswamedha.'
It is for the glory of God, the good of India, and
the honour of England that this atrocity has come to
an end. It has long ceased, and both we and the
people seem almost to have forgotten that it was once
a horror daily perpetrated ; but if England had done
nothing more for India than suppressed suttee and
greatly diminished infanticide, she could well claim
the admiration and gratitude of the civilized world.

NOTE.

The editor of Rammohun Roy's English works says, 'In a great
many instances the suttee was the victim of her greedy relatives, and
in more, of rash words spoken in the first fit of grief, and of the vanity
of her kindred, who considered her shrinking from the first resolve an
indelible disgrace. Many a horrible murder was thus committed, the
cries and shrieks of the poor suttee being drowned by the sound of
tom-toms, and her struggles made powerless by her being pressed down
by bamboos.'

An able writer in a Calcutta journal, reviewing such portions of
Sir Henry S. Maine's book on *Ancient Village Communities* as relate
to the laws of inheritance, says, ' Sir Henry Maine's inquiry as to the
reasons which have led to the unfavourable position of Hindu women,
is a deeply interesting one. The Hindu wife had, theoretically, more
ample rights of property than those accorded to married women either
by the Roman jurists or by the Common Law of England. During
her husband's life, the Hindu codes secured to her a larger independence
in the exercise of those rights. After his death, she succeeded, if
childless, to the life-rent of his whole property. Whence came it that
a class of persons with so high a legal status fell into the condition in

which the Anglo-Indian courts found the women of this country? How did it happen that a system of jurisprudence which showed so great a tenderness to the proprietary rights of women, proved so indifferent to their life? What explanation can be given of this ample independence of women as regards their property co-existing with the most cruel disregard of their personal sufferings; of *Stridhan*, or the liberally conceived separate estate of the Hindu wife, appearing side by side with *Sati*, or the burning of the Hindu widow?

'The answer given by Sir Henry Sumner Maine is a deeply suggestive one. Many earnest Englishmen are at present labouring to improve the chances of their countrywomen in the struggle for existence. Some of the projects by which they have proposed to accomplish this object would, in the opinion of thoughtful lookers-on, force women into a position for which they are not suited by the fundamental facts of human life, a position that they would not be able to maintain, and one which, by placing them in harsh competition with the other sex, would, on the whole, injure, rather than improve, their practical condition. The immediate social value of Sir Henry Maine's chapter on Hindu women consists in this, that it shows how an experiment of a similar sort has already been tried, and how it has failed. Hindu institutions, at some early period in their history, gave to women a proprietary independence more ample than Hindu society in its later development found convenient. The ancient law came down with the sanction of religion, and could not be formally repealed.

'But the Bráhmans, who administered it, found means to defeat its intent. These sacerdotal jurists deemed it very unsuitable that a childless widow should step into her husband's whole property for life. The proper use for such an estate they held to consist in expenditure on religious ceremonies for the benefit of the dead, and women could not, according to their system, conduct these rites. It is true that the most liberal of commentators denies that *all* a dead man's property is intended for religious uses, and points out certain acts of a *quasi*-religious character, which a woman can properly perform—such as digging tanks. But, generally speaking, the whole influence of the priestly and legal professions was arrayed against the extensive proprietary rights which the ancient Hindu law had conferred on women. In like manner the male members of a family looked with a grudging eye on the young widow who excluded them from her husband's estate. Neither the Bráhmans, nor the collateral relatives, could alter the law, but they discovered that they might defeat it by getting rid of the woman. Self-immolation, which finds no authority in the Vedas, was urged upon widows ; a sacred text was corrupted, so as to give it the sanction of a religious duty ; and the whole influence of the Bráhmans and collateral male relatives was brought to bear on the unhappy victim at the moment when a recent sorrow had rendered her indifferent to life.

'This detestable practice, whatever its remote origin, received its development from the conflict which had thus taken place between "the liberality of Hindu institutions to females at some long past period of their development, and the dislike towards this liberality manifested by the Brahminical lawyers," and by the male collateral relatives. In Bengal proper, the liberality of the law had been carried to its furthest extent, and, to use the words of Sir Henry Maine, "a considerable portion of the soil of the wealthiest Indian province is in the hands of childless widows, as tenants for life. But it was exactly in Bengal proper that the English, on entering India, found widow-burning not merely an occasional, but a constant and almost universal, practice among the wealthier classes ; and, as a rule, it was only the childless widow, and never the widow with minor children, who burnt herself on her husband's pyre. There is no question that there was the closest connection between the law and the religious custom, and that the widow was made to sacrifice herself in order that her tenancy for life might be got out of the way."

'The Hindu law, in short, gave to woman a status which Hindu society found it inconvenient to maintain, and the weakest went to the wall.'

When Sir Charles Napier was in charge of a feudatory state in the North-West of India, he dealt with widow immolation in a very summary, conclusive manner. Preparations were being made for a suttee, and Sir Charles objected. 'But,' said a high native official, with equal politeness and assurance, 'this is a religious rite—a most sacred one—which must not be interfered with.' 'Yes,' replied Sir Charles, 'and we have a custom that any one who burns women alive must be hung.' The immolation did *not* take place.

A BIBLE CART IN NORTH INDIA.

(*From an electro supplied by the Zenana Bible and Medical Mission.*)

CHAPTER IX.

WIDOWHOOD.

ACCORDING to the Indian Census Report for 1891, the population had reached the immense total of 287,223,331. Of these 146,727,296 were males, and 140,496,135 females. Of the former 6,412,483 were widowers, whilst of the latter no less than 22,657,429 were widows. Of these 13,878 were under 4 years of age ; 64,040 between 5 and 9 ; 174,532 between 10 and 14 ; 4,160,548 between 15 and 34 ; 6,996,592 between 35 and 49 ; 11,224,933, 50 and over ; and 22,906 whose age was not returned.

These figures are most suggestive, since they differ in almost every feature from what is found in every European state.

In Europe there are about 2500 widows to every 1000 widowers ; in India the proportion of the former rises to about 3570. It will be noticed that almost one-sixth of the entire female population are widows.[1]

[1] 'A serious development of the Brahminic system, indicated in some of the census reports, is the tendency in the present day of peace and plenty to manifest their prosperity, firstly by prohibiting the

This arises from three causes: early marriage, the universality of marriage, and enforced widow-hood.[1]   In many parts of South India, thirty-three per cent. of the Brahmin women are widows.   Some of

marriage of widows, and then by insisting upon carrying out strictly the Brahminic injunction, and save themselves from the place to which the law-maker consigns them, by getting all their girls married before they have reached womanhood. Many cases have occurred within recent years to show that any movement among the literate classes in the direction of the abrogation of these two precepts is but mouth deep, whilst their heart is with the observance of them to the utmost. *Longum iter per precepta, breve et efficace per exempla;* but when opportunities occur for carrying into practice amongst them-selves or their families some of the reforms they have been so strenu-ously endeavouring to impose upon others, it is remarkable to note what an amount of filial piety, and of deference to the feelings of those to whom their respect is due, comes into play, to prevent them from becoming martyrs to their principles. On the other hand, amongst the castes below the Brahmin and Rajput, who have no education, and make no pretence of being sensible of any defects in their social system, we find continual attempts to conquer society by proving their claim to recognition through the adoption of these very tokens of high rank, which, by the admission of many who observe them, are blots on the social arrangements of the community, which it is the duty of men of light and leading to suppress. Thus, whilst the mouth is proclaim-ing its enlightenment and progress, the trunk is waddling backwards as fast as the nature of the ground will permit.'—*Census Report for* 1891, p. 260.

[1] 'The universality of marriage, in the leading province of Bengal, is very striking among women. Taking the lives of 100 girls from the cradle to the grave; at the age of 10, 88 will be single, and 12 married; at 30 the same proportions nearly are maintained, but they are twisted round, for 87 are married, 12 widows, and 1 unmarried; at 60 there are no spinsters, but there are 87 widows, and 12 married women. The thorough and complete succession of the three stages of conjugal condition is striking. Half the girls who marry do so between 10 and 19, but the boys marry much later—two-thirds of all males, marrying at all, having been married between 20 and 29.'

the lowest castes recognize social unions with widows, but they are not celebrated with the same ceremonies as the first marriages, nor regarded with the same respect. They are a kind of civil contract ratified by the members of the caste, and though not accompanied by the elaborate religious ceremonies of a first marriage, are held to be a formal and legal union, which without the concurrence of the *punchayat* or representative caste committee, they would not be.

But in the upper castes no widow marriage is recognized. English law holds such marriages, duly solemnized, to be valid, but Hindu opinion and practice does not. A widow re-married, however suitably in age, rank, and circumstances, immediately loses her caste ; and the act deprives her of the respect and association of her parents, brothers, sisters, and caste people generally ; though probably no such result would follow on the clearest evidence of scandalous sin.

The prejudice against such marriages is intense beyond conception. It is no doubt slowly abating wherever English and Christian ideas are gaining power ; and the usages associated with widowhood have always been modified here and there, by love and pity ; nevertheless, they have had, and even yet have, intense force, and among a people so callous, so bound by custom, and so entirely resolved to acquiesce in what to them seems the conditions of destiny, it could not be but that the lot of widows would be most pitiable. It may, indeed, be safely asserted that the habitual condition of no class of human beings has been more so.

The rights of a widow to property are considerable, but she has hardly any other. Anyhow and anywhere a woman is not a free agent, and especially so if she be a widow. If her husband dies early, she remains in her father's house, or, if childless or with very young children, she will probably return to it; otherwise, she remains in the family of her late husband. In the former instance, there is the probability of some alleviation to her sorrows. Natural affection and womanly pity will flow out in sympathy, and ease, as far as may be, the heavy burden laid by inexorable custom on her tender life. But anyhow her state is pitiable. It is so, not only because of its physical conditions. As we have seen, the lot of a married woman is generally cheerless and restricted. But if her husband die, the small amount of respect she has had as a wife and mother ceases, for not only does general sentiment turn against her, she is exposed to a series of pains and penalties such as no other large class of women have ever had to endure.

Her troubles begin on the day of her husband's death, for along with the lamentations of his family are mingled reproaches and even curses and execrations on her. Then may begin, and probably does, to continue all through life, the following usages :—

The *tahli*, a symbol hung round the neck of a bride

by her husband at the time of marriage, and answering somewhat to our wedding ring, is taken away. Her long, carefully cherished hair, regarded as her greatest natural ornament, and dressed carefully every day, is cut clean off, and she must be shaven every ten days. On her forehead certain vermilion marks, indicative of the glory of the married state, must no more appear. Her pleasant attire is taken away, and replaced by coarse common clothing, without border, fringe, or trace of beauty. Her numerous ornaments, so dear to her foolish, ignorant mind, never taught to prize higher and better things, are taken away, perhaps torn off her person by violence. She is made a household drudge. She is expected to get up early, before the servants of the family. No one will supply her with water, she must go to the well and fetch it for herself. It is unlucky to meet her. She is supposed to be in eternal mourning for her deceased lord, though she may never have seen him except at her child-wedding. In short, she suffers a living death. She must bathe on a different day from married women. She must not sleep on a pleasant and easy couch ; she must have but one meal in the day, and that of coarse fare ; and twice during each month she must neither eat nor drink during the twenty-four hours. If there is a wedding or other festival in the house, it is best that she should not be present, lest, like a planet of evil omen, she bring her own ill fortune into the lot of others. An evil destiny is supposed to cleave to her ; she herself

I

is held to be subject to malign influences, and may possibly transmit them to others.

The treatment of widows arises from two deeply rooted ideas, each of them powerful enough to affect all the conditions of life in any society by which they are received—a belief in transmigration, and a settled assumption that women are altogether inferior and subordinate to men.

Transmigration is far more than a belief with the great mass of the people. Whether owing to the vividness of their imaginations, natural distrust, intense religiousness, the profusion of all forms of life around them, the tremendous power with which the forces of nature act, or a combination of these, the Hindus accept unquestioningly this weird belief, which strongly influences all their thoughts, feelings, and actions. What they may become depends far more on what they are and have been, and on caste observances relating to what is eaten, and physical contact and association, than on moral integrity and purity. The Brahmin expects to be a divine man in a future birth because he is a Brahmin now, and punctilious on all questions relative to food and touch, though he lives in the habitual violation of every moral duty. But to eat beef, to partake of food with a European, or even with a Hindu Sudra, entails degradation of being through numerous forms of existence! Then, too, whilst it is very easy to fall, it is very difficult to rise.

Through these causes it is that every typical Hindu

has an intense suspicion and dread lest he should lose
his caste, which he may do unconsciously, and through
no fault whatever of his own, and hence be born a
woman, a Sudra, a pariah, or even a toad or a jackal,
in a future birth. What he now is, and whatever
happens to him that to an important extent affects
his prosperity, is assumed to spring out of the condition of soul thus inherited from a previous birth. For
a wife, therefore, to lose her husband is considered conclusive evidence that an evil destiny clings to her, and
now, perhaps for the hundredth time, hurls her down
to misery. She is, therefore, not commiserated, but
abhorred, dreaded, and condemned. All this is very
illogical, irrational, and inconsequent, but it is Hindu
sentiment struggling ardently, honestly, though
blindly, to interpret the mystery of being. And it
assists us best and most charitably to understand the
mingled dread and dislike with which widows are
regarded. A son is the dearest possession of a family ;
but should he die, it is assumed, especially by the
ignorant, superstitious women of the family, which
usually means all of them, that this has happened as
a part of his wife's evil destiny ; not as punishment
to the deceased husband or to the members of his
family, but to her. But her evil destiny is their
misfortune. Had he not married *her*, this would not
have happened to him. Therefore she is abhorred,
degraded in person, made the drudge of the house,
and reproached with such terms of scorn as only
superstitious and ignorant women can use.

And a most potent element in the Hindu disposition lends itself either to inflict suffering in such cases, or to be indifferent to its infliction. No race is more

HINDU GIRL.
(*From an electro supplied by the Zenana Bible and Medical Mission.*)

ready to acknowledge a divine or supernatural power in human affairs and to submit absolutely to destiny. Let a Hindu arrive at the conclusion—which he very readily does—that an event is according to destiny,

destiny being above and superior even to the will of God—he accepts it with a submissiveness which Christian resignation seldom approaches. If a wife

THE SAME AFTER THREE YEARS' CHRISTIAN TRAINING.
(*From an electro supplied by the Zenana Bible and Medical Mission.*)

becomes a widow, he assumes that she should suffer, that he is working with destiny to allow her to suffer, and that to make her happy or honoured would be impious, because an attempt to evade the workings of

destiny, and therefore possibly bring on himself a
malign influence, from the supernatural forces by
which he believes all life is surrounded. There may
be a great lack of reasonableness in this, but he does
not reason too closely, though he thinks much, and
imagines still more. Then, if it be considered that
Hindu women are not only intensely ignorant but
profoundly superstitious, it will be seen how easy it is
for them to be passive at the degraded state of their
widowed sisters, or even active in assisting to degrade
them.

Further, widowhood and its hard conditions are
based on the deeply rooted idea that a woman by
nature is inferior and subordinate to man. For her
to aspire to equality would be thought improper,
presumptuous, and almost impious. Even if she be
gifted, and her husband be intellectually and morally
debased, she must be in all things subordinate to him.
To recognize his superiority is her highest virtue ; she
exists only for him. When he dies, her use in life is
ended. For her to marry a second time is regarded
as unnatural, a violation of all that is proper and even
decent. She has fulfilled her destiny, henceforth she
is not even a flower born to blush unseen, but a
broken branch left to wither and die. This is the
intense sentiment which governs society in its treatment of widows. I call it intense, for nothing short
of this can explain the perpetuation, among a race
naturally gentle, of a custom so irrational, so widespread, so inconvenient, and so calculated powerfully

to affect and influence the life and imagination, and
productive of so much evil and crime. It is the cause
of more heart-break and hopeless sorrow than any
one custom among mankind. For we must take into
account, first, the systematic and most humiliating
features of repression to which widows are subject;
then the sternness of the custom, dooming as it does
to hopeless widowhood mere children, who though
married, never lived with their husbands ; and, finally,
the immense number who are doomed to such a life.
Think of it : 22,600,000 women of all ages, from even
the tender child of five, thus thought of, and multitudes
of them leading such a life! But it is out of our
power to understand what this stupendous number
signifies ; a few illustrations will assist to bring it more
within our comprehension. It means one in six of
the entire female population. It means almost as
many widows in India as there are men, women, and
children in all England, with only Lancashire left
out. And of these, 252,000 are under 15 years of
age ; that is, as many girl-widows as there are people
of both sexes and all ages in Bristol or Nottingham,
or Bradford or Edinburgh. Think of what all this
signifies ! [1]

And widows are powerless. Custom, society, public
sentiment, are passive or unfriendly. If she is yet a
child in her father's house, or if after bereavement she
return to it, pity and affection may shield her from
some of the cruelest effects of superstition and

[1] *Westminster Review*, 1891, p. 118.

custom. So, too, this may happen if her loss comes later in life, after she has gained influence, and her children are sufficiently old and well trained to protect and shield her; especially will this be so if she has sons, for though looked on as a sinner, her lot will be alleviated on account of her being the mother of the superior sex. But these conditions may be wanting, and in every case social and public sentiment are against her.

How did such peculiar usages originate and become so intense? Indian ideas of marriage are based on conceptions different from those held elsewhere. The object of marriage in the East is primarily religious. ' Viewed from the woman's side, it is—(1) that she may have some male in whose rear she may walk into heaven, for her own good deeds gain her no entrance there, or (2) if she has no brothers, that the said male may lead the family procession within the gates. Viewed from the father's side, it is that he may leave behind him some one to pray his soul out of hell ' (*Putt*), and offer sacrifices to the supernal and infernal deities. A male descendant only can do this, and so regnant is this idea that every other consideration has become subordinate to it. The wife is only esteemed as the mother of the son. She is supposed to belong sacramentally to one husband, in such a manner that she must never belong to another. A father in selecting a wife for his son will prefer one out of a family in which boys are more frequently born than girls, and avoid one in which widowhood is frequent; for next to the loss of caste the prevalence of girls and widows in a family are regarded as the greatest misfortunes. It is considered unlucky for women to see the face of a widow before seeing any other object in the morning, and most men would postpone any business on which they were setting out if their path were crossed by a widow. Their persons, their state, their names are held in contempt. The name *rand* by which they are generally designated, is the same that is generally given to a nautch girl or a harlot. 'Every town, every village, almost every house is full of widows who are debarred from all amusements, and, if childless, converted into household drudges. They often lead bad lives. Their lives, like those of lepers, are as a living death, and they would often give themselves up to be burned alive, if the law would let them. The spirit of Sati still survives.'[1]

The influence of her position on the widow must be most disastrous. Credible report states that multitudes are driven or drawn to a life of sin. But if she has any power of imagination and thought, how must she regard herself? She is abhorred or despised or pitied by all she knows. There is no hope for her : a widow she must remain to the bitter end. She is ignorant of books and learning, shut out from all knowledge of the opinions and thoughts of the outer world. She is deeply superstitious, and religious in

---

[1] Sir M. M. Williams' *Modern India*, p. 78 ; *Census of India*, 1891, chap. ix.

her way, taking it for granted that many gods are vengeful and malignant, and that destiny rules the lot of all. She has become a widow—that is, either she did something, or failed to do something, ages ago, which has brought her under evil and malignant influences, and which may pursue her through many births or states of being; or some lapse or failure in this life has brought this evil on her. She connects what she is with what she has been and done, concluding that she is under a ban and curse, pursued by evil either in the form of an implacable divinity or an unfeeling irresistible force, it would be as vain as it would be impious to oppose. Every one around her thinks on these lines, and regards her as an accursed being to whom cleaves misfortune and misery. From her childhood this is how she has been habituated to look at all people and things; she has never heard anything else; she has no chance of knowing anything else; she has never been taught to think or to reason. If she has ever ventured openly to do so, she has most likely been told, in no veiled words, that she is only a woman, and that it is her part to submit and obey, and not presume to think for herself. I can imagine, out of perdition, nothing so moving and pathetic as the conflicting terror, fear, loathing, and despair of such a woman. Is it surprising if numbers of such sink into imbecility or insanity, or commit suicide, or turn to a life of shame? Her state is but too accurately described in the lines—

'And death and life she hated equally,
And nothing saw for her despair,
But dreadful time, dreadful eternity,
No comfort anywhere.'

Such a state of society as this presents may seem almost incredible, and not a few Hindus say and write a good deal in an apologetic and faint-hearted manner in excuse, if not in vindication of the status and treatment of women generally. But five facts are clear—

1. The general drift of Hindu sentiment, as expressed in all ancient writings, is unjust and injurious to women.

2. The ruling features of female infanticide, early marriage, perpetual widowhood, suttee, and subordination have more or less prevailed in purely native society from remote times.

3. There is the general admission, on the part of the great majority of unprejudiced, educated men, that the entire system of native sentiment and usage relating to female society, needs to be revised and reformed.

4. Every educated Hindu woman in modern life whose voice has been heard, declares the condition of her sex to be most unjust, injurious, and heart-breaking.

5. There is the almost uniform testimony of European and American men and women, who are competent to express an opinion, to the same effect.

A remarkable book was privately circulated in

Bombay in 1890, called *The Story of a Widow Re-marriage; being the Experiences of Madhowdas Rugnathdas, Merchant of Bombay.* Mr. Rugnathdas, a widower, forty-three years of age, of good caste and social rank, married a widow suitable in rank, family, and age; and this is how the news of her marriage was received in the bride's family. 'Her mother and grandmother, her sister and sister-in-law, and all the rest of the friends and relatives, joined in a chorus of cries. The women beat their breasts and foreheads, and the demonstrations of grief were loud enough to startle the whole neighbourhood. Her poor mother and other near relatives were inconsolable. They could never have dreamt that the news could have been so very bad. Nothing could persuade them to touch food. The house was filled with gloom.'

And then followed for eighteen years, up to the time the book was written, a series of attempts to boycott, ruin, and annoy Mr. Rugnathdas and his wife, which, but for ample evidence, would be incredible. They were threatened with violence, put out of caste, maligned to European society; systematic attempts were made to ruin Mr. Rugnathdas as a banker and merchant; and, strangest and saddest of all, though they lived happily together, and in all the relations of life were virtuous and honourable, their relatives were implacable, and early friends, who professed, advanced, and in theory advocated, widow-marriage, withdrew their friendship, and in some instances were hostile, though knowing well, and admitting in private, that enforced widowhood was the cause of endless sorrow and crime, the weak,' timid excuse being, 'The time is not yet come for widow re-marriage. At least fifty years must elapse before the time will be ripe for it.' The book is a pathetic illustration of Hindu character and the singular difficulty of introducing any reforms, however rational and humane.

The dreadful sentence said by Dante to be written over the portals of hell—

'All hope abandon, ye who enter here'—

describes the state of widowhood in the long ages of the past. But now, happily, the dawning of a better time is perceptible. The thick darkness which has for many centuries rested on the fortunes of these tens of millions of gentle, graceful women is being lifted. But it will be long, far longer than is usually supposed, before the day breaks and the shadows flee away ; for how few adequately understand what a stupendous task it is to change the ideas and customs of a vast and ancient Asiatic race ! But the beginning of the end is seen. The people are beginning to realize the evils of their own usages.

About fifty years ago, Motee Lal Seal, a well-known resident in Calcutta, knowing well the power of example over his countrymen and their excessive timidity, offered a thousand pounds to any respectable Hindu who would marry a widow, and no one claimed the tempting sum !

In 1856 the Indian Government passed an Act

removing all legal obstacles to the marriage of widows. But though the law is favourable, and public sentiment declares that widows should be humanely treated and their marriage encouraged, and societies have been formed to advocate such views and encourage these marriages, it is surprising to think how little, at least in the latter direction, has been done.[1] Nowhere does sentiment run so far ahead of practice as in India. Nevertheless, the leaven of the new ideas is powerfully at work, and as they have reason, humanity, and social good on their side, the new ideas must finally be victorious.[2]

[1] 'It is in reality, however, a dead letter, as the Hindus regard it with abhorrence, and have not mitigated in the least their strenuous opposition to the re-marriage of the widow. Thirty years after its enactment only about sixty re-marriages are reported in all India. It was a generation or more in advance of native opinion, which, however, at the present time is beginning to agitate for larger liberty in the matter' (*The Missionary Review* for March, 1898, p. 200).

[2] The ideas governing the status of women described in this chapter are common to the Hindu race; but the enforcement of the customs and usages varies with the caste and nationality of the people. What I have written applies most closely to the extensive and populous province of Bengal. But the usages described are most enforced—as easily they can be—in high caste and well-to-do families. In some instances the severity of daily discipline on a widow is mitigated in the case of children of tender years. In others the heartless and almost savage manner in which a widow is initiated into her forlorn state by tearing off her ornaments, shaving her head, and otherwise degrading her, are not enforced, and among the lower castes everywhere, as we have stated, instances are found of widows living with widowers, under imperfect religious and social sanction. Such unions, though dissolved at pleasure, are mutually convenient, and an escape, as by a back door, from the evils of widowhood; they are therefore indulgently regarded by a people who, whilst intolerant of any violations of caste-purity, are lax on most questions relating to chastity.

A ZENANA LADY IN BENGAL.

CHAPTER X.

THE EVILS ARISING OUT OF THE STATUS OF WOMEN.

THE great domestic and social evils of Hindu life are beginning to be recognized by the people themselves, though pride of race and an intensely conservative habit of thought, lead them to minimize such evils and be half-hearted in any attempts to remove them. Those evils have never been adequately described; they are too far-reaching, and touch too closely and tenderly the entire structure of native society, with its mystery, reticence, and distrust, to be understood by any ordinary observer. There are few Hindus who could or would give a candid portraiture of native domestic life, and no one of Western race, however well acquainted with the facts, has the knowledge, or can have, of the inner life of the women of India requisite to enable us to understand what it is. Possibly some Hindu lady in the near future, possessed of ample knowledge, and with adequate courage, candour, and descriptive power, may give this to the world; and when it is done it will bring to missionary and benevolent effort tenfold zeal, sympathy, and aid. But the *facts*, so far as known, should awaken the profoundest interest and sympathy of Christian women toward their Indian sisters.

1. That great *physical evils* arise out of early marriage, and other customs in a lesser degree, can easily be imagined. Every medical man of sufficient experience, and all ladies who as doctors or nurses have access to native families, declare that disease, ill health, and delicacy of constitution are unusually prevalent. The possibilities—nay, even probabilities—of family life, when wives are ten or twelve years of age, have recently been brought under public notice in instances of revolting crime, and shown the need of a

great change in early marriage relations. But ever since child marriage became customary—how many hundreds of years ago none can tell—such tragedies have been possible, and doubtless have occurred in tens of thousands of cases, before humaner sentiments began to prevail, and when there were no British tribunals to take cognizance of such sins against humanity.

But besides the probability of a violent death through this custom, we must take account of the immense amount of suffering and disease, often ending only with life, it has caused. The facts brought to light, and the evidence of medical and other authorities, have roused public attention to this evil, and led, happily, after much agitation, to a change in the law, raising the age of consent from ten to twelve years—the law and the necessity for it all too plainly revealing the unsatisfactory, repellent features of early married life.

And one evil produces another. What is likely to be the *physical* state of both mother and child, when the former herself may be but a child thirteen or fourteen years of age, and even more a child in all true knowledge, and be the mother of a large family ere she is twenty years of age ? It is well known to all familiar with native society that, generally graceful, and often beautiful as Hindu girls are, they cease to be either at thirty, and are even old at forty ; and reliable report states that delicacy of constitution, ill health and disease are very common. And this is

K

inevitable, not only because of premature maternity, the most ignorant midwifery, and the physically ruinous and cruel treatment to which a mother is exposed through the caste usages, which separate her for many days from the small comforts of the family, but also from the want of air, exercise, and change of scene. To the great mass of women belonging to the middle and upper classes good physical exercise is not practicable. The roof of a house, a verandah, or a small yard or garden, are the only places accessible to them. Even where the area is greater, the monotony of treading it day by day and year by year, seeing only the same few faces and gazing on the same scene, often only a patch of the sky or a dull courtyard, or an ill-cultivated garden, must be most depressing and detrimental to health. There must be many myriads of women who have never since childhood enjoyed a good walk or ride, or gazed on any scene which did not lie between their husband's and their father's house, multitudes of them for years never leaving the house in which they are immured.

2. And *moral evil* ensues.

Marriage is an engrossing topic in all feminine conversation. And there is little reserve in the manner in which it is spoken of. The people have in some directions a delicate sense of propriety, but it does not extend to questions relating to marriage. Native servants, even, will talk to English little children of their courtships, weddings, and future husbands and wives with a freedom which to us is shocking and indecent, but which they are surprised to hear is so.

Among themselves, since they have so little to think and talk of, and marriage, especially to women, being the most exciting and important event in life, the occasion when they receive public recognition, it is not surprising that it should absorb their attention and be a topic for incessant talk. But what must be the effect on the minds of boys and girls, not even in their teens, when their marriages are talked about in their presence in no veiled terms ; when from her fifth year a girl is taught habitually to pray for a good husband, who will love her, who may live long, never take a second wife, and that she may be the mother, not of daughters, but of many sons ; and the boy of seven or eight, who is taken from school for three weeks or a month to be married with elaborate cere- monies, great festivity, indecent speech, to a child of yet more tender age he has never before seen ? Can there be any wonder the little ones grow up to be deficient in intellectual force and physical stamina, through having their minds absorbed in affairs of which they should know nothing ?

3. Social evil ensues, and that in many ways.

A boy who marries a girl can neither support him- self nor his wife, nor can he in any true sense care for and protect her. He and she for years must be dependent on his parents or hers, and possibly their children also. As they are dependent, they must be subject to others, and this is so especially with the wife, who is far more dependent on her mother or sister-in-law than on her own husband or parents. Thus there intervenes, from the time of marriage, grave obstacles to the husband and wife being one in affection, sympathy or interest. Three illustrative instances may be quoted here :—

'When examining *a girl of sixteen* for some skin trouble, I noticed a large scar which covered almost entirely the sole of her left foot. On inquiry I heard a sad tale. The girl was brought up in a happy home, but after marriage the illtreatment she received at her husband's often made her run away to her own sweet home. One day, finding no kind of punishment would cure the girl of this habit, the husband and his mother tied the girl to a pole, and mercilessly branded her foot with a hot iron ; but the girl managed to run away within two days to her mother, who carried her on her back to a hospital in Bombay. The police took up the case, and got the husband sentenced to three years' rigorous imprisonment. After his release, she would be afraid to go to him, for fear of losing her life. In this land of idolatry and immorality, with no education, would it be strange if this girl falls into the crooked path ?

'Another young girl was brought to me in a strange way. Although the girl was suffering from a bad fever, yet the mother-in-law would neither give her medicine nor consent to her going to her parents. The girl had to eat stale food, do the grinding, and had only a mat on the damp floor to lay her weary and feverish

HOSPITAL GROUP, DOCTORS AND NURSES (LUCKNOW).

(From an electro supplied by the Zenana Bible and Medical Mission.)

body at night. Knowing that the girl would accompany her younger brother-in-law to a festival, the father on that day waited on the road, and on seeing her brought her at once to the dispensary. I found her quite emaciated, and marks of violence were seen on her back. Her father—a frail little man—was so agitated that he was shivering from head to foot. I had to give him some medicine to soothe his nerves. The mother-in-law made a great row, took away her ornaments, and notified a lawyer. If the friends succeed in settling this affair, the girl will return to her husband after two or three years, or he will marry another girl. It is hard for me to relate to you such heart-rending tales, but I must, in order that you should know the deplorable state of women here. Christ alone can bring liberty and joy into such homes.'[1]

'Some months ago the wife of a man in one of the villages near Baharwa was ill. Mrs. Brown went to see her, and said she looked wretched, just lying out on her *parkom*, and with no extra clothing save her *sari*. She could not eat, so Mrs. Brown told her husband that she would give her some milk if he would send for it.

'"Oh, who should I send ?" he asked.

'" Come yourself."

'" I have the buffaloes to see to when they come in."

'" But after that ?"

'" Then there are the children to see to."

'" Well, send your daughter."

---

[1] Mrs. Doctor V. Karmarkar, Bassim, Bombay, Dec., 1895.

' "Oh, she cooks the evening meal."

'And so no one came for the milk.

'A few days after, at evening-time, I saw this poor woman's body carried out into the fields, and soon bright flames leapt up, and I knew it was being burnt. She had gone ; and last week, when at that village, I saw the new wife, who had already taken her place, and who was nursing the wee baby she had left behind.' [1]

And marriage always involves a *great expenditure of money*, which in many cases means a heavy burden of debt. The poorest parents, as well as the richest, spend extravagantly on weddings. Even the poor will spend a sum equal to half a year's wages, and the rich tens of thousands of rupees ; and since all classes are improvident, the money has often to be borrowed at a usurious rate of interest, which impoverishes the family for years. Custom demands this folly, and though parents know what it involves, and groan at the prospect, pride and cowardice induce them to submit to the evil. This undoubtedly was one great cause of infanticide. To be quit of a daughter was not only to be saved much trouble, but an inevitably heavy expense, out of all proportion to the parents' means.

Such customs are among the great causes why so many families, once wealthy and powerful, have now declined, and why indebtedness, with all its evils humiliations, and temptations to crime, so abounds.

---

[1] *India's Women*, Dec., 1892.

4. The evils flowing from the heterogeneous assembling of so many variously related persons, bound together by social ties and caste relations, but diverse in usage, sympathy, interest, cannot but be great. They have varying interests, and nothing to attract their minds toward higher affairs, or to train them to be forbearing, self-controlled, and unselfish. The men are little different, and morally no better. What temptations there must be in such families towards envy, jealousy, strife, and intrigue ! There is the evidence of a lady most competent to speak, and although her remarks apply specially to the influence of Islam in Mahomedan lands, they are applicable to Buddhist and Hindu countries also.

'They (false faiths) degrade women with an infinite degradation. I have lived in zenanas, and harems, and have seen the daily life of the secluded women, and I can speak from bitter experience of what their lives are—the intellect dwarfed, so that the woman twenty or thirty years of age is more like a child of eight intellectually ; while all the worst passions of human nature are stimulated and developed in a fearful degree ; jealousy, envy, murderous hate, intrigue, running to such an extent that in some countries I have hardly ever been in a woman's house or near a woman's tent without being asked for drugs with which to disfigure the favourite wife, to take away her life, or to take away the life of the favourite wife's infant son. This request has been made of me nearly two hundred times. This is only an indication of

TEACHING IN A ZENANA.

(*From an electro supplied by the Zenana Bible and Medical Mission.*)

the daily life, of whose miseries we think so little, and
which is a natural product of the systems that we
ought to have subverted long ago.' [1]

5. *National or race life suffers.*—India is more
suggestive of great problems to the philosopher,
philanthropist, and historian than any other country.
And one of these is how a great race, probably more
numerous for a thousand years than the population
of the Roman Empire at its zenith; most richly
dowered with intellectual and artistic gifts, and placed
where nature is most prolific and beneficent, should
have been unprogressive for centuries, never really
united into one great empire or confederation of
states, but subject all through the ages of credible
history, to the partial domination of first one and then
another of its more martial nationalities, Rajputs,
Mahrattas, or Punjabis ; or to foreigners whose presence is disliked, whose lack of caste defiles, and
whose religions have very little in common with their
own.   Whence this weakness, this repeated and continuous subjugation ?   Undoubtedly, one important
factor in the solution of this problem is the generally
low opinion held of women, and the corresponding
status to which they have been degraded.   Any one
familiar with all that is sung and said of women,
wives, and home, in the dramatic, lyric, and patriotic
literature of Rome, Israel, and Western Europe, will
recognize how much the courage, strength, and virtue
of their races have been associated with the place

[1] Mrs. Isabella Bishop.

they have given to women, and the respect in which they have been held. Manu gave expression to a deep truth when he said, 'When female relatives are made miserable, the family soon wholly perishes; but that family where they are not unhappy ever prospers.' But the text which follows suggests a base motive and a low estimate of the sex even at that early age—'Hence men who seek their own welfare should always honour women on holidays and festivals with gifts of ornaments, clothes, and dainty food.' The policy suggested indicates an imperfect, if not low idea of the tastes of women. It assumes that they are but children of a larger growth, who are to be petted and managed by indulgence rather than treated and trained as rational beings. As the method is injurious to a child, so is it to wives and husbands alike, and, where everything runs into system, to the whole community.

6. The unwise treatment of women has *reacted on men.*

The suspicion, fear, tyranny, and contempt, mingled with indulgence, with which they have long regarded women, have tended to make these qualities inherent parts of the national character. They mark the bearing of man towards man; of caste towards caste; of nationalities toward nationalities; of Bengali toward Rajput, of Hindustani toward Mahratta; of each, indeed, toward all others, and of all who have caste toward all who have it not. Hindus have great qualities, and a reserve of capabilities that will give them a foremost place in the future of the world's history ; but it will not be, cannot be, and would be a calamity to human nature if it were to be, before their entire system of domestic life were revolutionized and reformed.

Evil is wrought in another way. Men have selfishly built up an intricate, monstrous system of sentiment and custom for the control of women, which has for its corner-stone the supremacy of man and the subordination of women ; and according to natural law, by which the nonuse or misuse of a faculty destroys or maims it, and the law of mental and moral retribution so surely at work in this life even, through which men reap as they sow, and nations rise or fall as they obey or violate the great laws of eternal righteousness, they are injured by what they have done to others. They selfishly and unjustly have dealt with one-half their race, and detriment has come to themselves. It has been as when some subtle poison has been taken which permeates the whole system. Men have brought themselves to believe, and have constrained women to accept the custom, if not the belief, that early marriage, seclusion, implicit obedience, ignorance of letters, and permanent widowhood are the proper conditions of feminine life ; thus, unwittingly but surely, lowering the tone and character of all national life, and causing there to be a wilderness where there should have been a garden, a desert where should ; have been springs of water, winter where should have been summer. For who can imagine the loss of wisdom, learning, and knowledge, of intelligence and skill, of happiness, sympathy, and helpfulness, of courage, endurance, and refinement, caused all through many centuries, by millions of women being left mentally and morally undeveloped and uneducated ? Despised, distrusted, treated as incapable of taking care of themselves, and taught that to be kept, as it were, under lock and key is their privilege and safety ; such treatment must inevitably tend to make them timid, helpless, and trivial. They are most affectionate as mothers, but how disqualified they must be to train, either physically or intellectually, their sons to be manly, courageous, and enduring ! If the half even be true of what we are taught to believe, of the power and influence of mothers on their children, and if the greater indebtedness of great men, consciously and unconsciously, to their mothers, rather than to their fathers, then we may well regret that the women of India are left so much in a state of nature, and that such training as they receive should be on mistaken and pernicious lines. Think of the wide difference between a mother educated or uneducated, respected or distrusted, and then the lack of all intellectual training of the women of India generation after generation ! It must be obvious that multiplied evils will ensue where social and domestic life are on so perverted a basis. The result cannot but be disastrous. It is so on the women themselves. It narrows and dulls their minds ; it makes them timid,

superstitious, helpless ; it hinders their usefulness
and efficiency; it degrades them ; it limits their
sources of enjoyment, and bars all progress. And
it is disastrous to men and families, for such women,
though sympathetic and affectionate, cannot be wise,
helpful, reliable companions to their husbands, or
exert over their children the moral and intellectual
influence requisite to make them wise, virtuous, well-
balanced, energetic members of society.[1]

7. The *seclusion and isolation* in which they are
kept is injurious.

This insulting and degrading usage goes to make
them what they are assumed to be ; for stripped of all
euphuisms, the customs have their root in the intense
distrust men have of men, and the suspicion that the
integrity of women is only to be secured by allowing
them no freedom, though they vainly assume that
privacy is a mark of their husbands' care and respectability. They are excessively restricted in what they
can hear and see—and thus are not only deprived of
pleasures that are perfectly innocent, but of influences
that are highly disciplinary and educational. So is
it a loss to them and to men that the two sexes, even
in the same house, dwell apart. Especially is the
fact disastrous to men. It fosters pride, conceit, and
ill manners. Left without the refining and restraining

---

[1] ' Especially do I want people to recognize that the women of our
Western Hemisphere represent the highest type of woman, greatly
owing to the respect and honour paid to them by men ; but that the
moment the honour and respect are diminished, the high type of
woman will vanish ' (Tennyson).

influences which always flow from the society of virtuous women, they become the more coarse, selfish, and unclean, in conduct, conversation, and character.

8. Evil produces evil. It is unnecessary to do more than call attention to the striking manner in which an original error in opinion and wrong in policy has led on to the great evils here laid bare. Women, it is assumed, are of an evil nature, and not to be trusted; therefore restrict their liberty and limit their influence, say the Shastras. Hence came child marriage, seclusion, and the discouragement of education. Then as children cannot choose their own partners, parents must select for them. But marriage was not easily brought about. It was difficult to find husbands, expensive to marry daughters, troublesome to take care of them ; hence came the disappointment with which the birth of a daughter is received, infanticide, perpetual widowhood, entailing on families a heavy expenditure and a great weight of watchfulness and solicitude ; and from these probably came the suggestion and certainly the encouragement of suttee. History gives us no instance of the subtle and widespread influence of mistaken opinion equal to this.

9. Think of the suffering and sorrow arising out of the status of women. Suffering and sorrow are nowhere so abundant as in heathen lands, and this is a fact the significance of which few sufficiently lay to heart. As Mrs. Isabella Bishop says of her extensive travels in Eastern lands, ' Wherever I have been, I have seen sin and sorrow and shame. There is an

infinite degradation of men. The whole continent of
Asia is corrupt. It is the scene of barbarities, tortures,
brutal punishments, oppression, official corruption,
which is worst under Mahomedan rule ; of all things
which are the natural products of systems which are
without God in Christ. There are no sanctities of
home ; nothing to tell of righteousness, temperance,
or judgment to come ; only a fearful looking for, in
the future, of fiery indignation from some quarter, they
know not what ; a dread of everlasting re-births into
forms of obnoxious reptiles or insects, or of tortures
which are infinite, and which are depicted in pictures
of fiendish ingenuity.'

'The dark places of the earth are full of the habita-
tions of cruelty.' 'Their sorrows are multiplied that
exchange the Lord for another god.' This was so
more than 2000 years ago, and it is equally so to-day,
because it is according to an eternal law. False
religion is neither productive of goodness nor happiness ; and whilst all Asia and Africa abound with the
evidences that it is so, the most obvious of all proof
is in the condition of Hindu women. Try to imagine
not only the possible but actual sorrow, suffering, and
heart-break that have come through long ages, and
that are coming even in our age, to millions of
daughters who, with the dawn of intellectual consciousness, learn that they are little better than a misfortune to their families, and less esteemed than their
brothers. Girls married to men they have never seen
or known ; wives not treated as equals, not trusted

with money or liberty or family affairs, and not even gently spoken to ; mothers who fear that the birth of a daughter may cause them to lose the affections of their husbands, disappointment to their family, reproach from their neighbours, and perhaps a second wife, to their humiliation and shame ;—to widows, hunger, thirst, disfigurement, reproach, scorn, and personal loathing. It is as well, perhaps, that we are slow to comprehend what all this means, for if we could but realize one-hundredth part of it, we should be deprived of rest and peace, if indeed our hearts were not broken. But to understand something of its extent and depth is salutary, since it makes us grateful for our national exemption from such a crushing weight of woe, and eager to remove the intolerable burden from the lives of those who now faint and fall beneath its weight. The greatest causes of human misery now at work in the world are war, intemperance, despotic government, slavery, and Hindu usages of women. I am inclined to think that none of them produce such an aggregate of human misery as the last. It affects more or less the lives, from beginning to end, of tens of millions of women, and that day by day all through life.

A SCHOOL IN NORTH INDIA.

CHAPTER XI.

THESE are worthy of close investigation, because of their peculiarities, and since they seem in many respects out of accord with some of the leading features of Hindu human nature.

Among an intelligent, courteous, gentle, placid, unemotional, and certainly not cruel race, it is singular that customs should have arisen and prevailed for centuries which press so heavily on the most gentle and attractive half of the race. These customs have been accepted for ages as implicitly as if they were laws of nature it would be hopeless if not impious to oppose, no instance being on record of a protest by any considerable number of people against any of these, on the ground of irrationality, injustice, or inhumanity. To Christianity solely belongs the honour of protest and practical action against them.

When a Hindu was asked if there were any points on which all, however sectarian, were agreed, he replied, 'Yes ; we all believe in the sanctity of the cow and the depravity of women.'

Hindu customs are the outcome of race characteristics and conditions, though the one often seem contradictory to the other. This is so everywhere, and on all such subjects it is important to notice how powerfully one passion or feature of character or sentiment, or a concurrence of circumstances, may modify and affect individual and even national character. Refinement and moral laxity, intemperance and good nature, pride and meanness, amiability and vice, manly virtues and one besetting sin go together. And every nation is swayed by some sentiment or enthralled by some usage which astonishes all others, and of which it is half ashamed. Religious sentiment, for instance, has over the Hindu race a power in everyday life such as it has not over any Western race. Any one wishing to understand the people and their ways will meet with paradoxes and incongruities, or things that seem so to the non-Aryan observer, and which he is inclined to regard at first as irrational, wondering how an intellectual and meditative race, more averse to destroy life than any other, can have come to adopt them, but which from the Hindu point of view seem rational, and even inevitable. Grant, for instance, the postulate, which has been accepted in all ages by all classes, male and female, learned and unlearned, that women are, through the subtle but inevitable laws of transmigration, inferior to men, intellectually and morally—so little able to take care of themselves, that they need ever to be dependent on men, and protected by them for their own safety and the well-being of families. Grant this, and all else that we see easily follows.

One continually finds, in the investigation of Oriental questions, that the people are not as bad as they seem, but, on the contrary, humane and rational. This is no reason why their opinions and usages should be accepted, but it is why their sentiments, and even prejudices, should be treated with respect, and they not misjudged and condemned—as too frequently they are—as cruel, vicious, and irrational. They are neither one nor the other, and it is evidence of this that invariably the better they are known by intelligent Europeans, the more they are respected and liked.

The customs, laws, and general condition of a people usually have their roots in their intellectual, moral, and emotional qualities. This is specially so with Eastern races, for they have been far less affected and modified by emigration, conquest, travel, and imitativeness than any of the nations of Southern and Western Europe. This is almost as true of the Hindus as of the Chinese. The former brought with them into India a consciousness of their own superiority over other races, a complacency in their own institutions, a religiousness of temperament—always an element of great strength—and an immobility of character which have given marked peculiarities to their institutions, and enabled them to resist external modifying forces with the silent, solid force

with which a granite mountain resists the waves of
the sea. The course of events which led them to
migrate from Central Asia tended to develop strong
and exclusive race qualities. Though they were
superior to the aborigines in all the arts of civilization—and evidently, from their old Vedic hymns and
songs, very conscious of their superiority—they had
ever to be watchful to preserve their supremacy as
conquerors and their hereditary purity as a race ;
and the assertion of such claims in these times of
struggle and danger depended, or was supposed to
depend, entirely on men. Whenever they received the
aborigines into their communities, it was not as equals,
but inferiors, doomed to hereditary subordination.

Thus an original pride of race and love of power
hardened into a system of domination and exclusive-
ness such as nowhere else has ever been seen. This
haughty and intense assumption of superiority in
opinion, and as far as practicable in position and
affairs, claimed for and finally secured for one class
over another an unchallenged right such as the world
has nowhere else seen : Hindu over every other race,
caste over no caste, Khetriya over Shudra, man over
woman, and Brahmin transcendently over all. These
became fixed ideas, which found expression in the
assumed divine laws and customs of the whole race,
and were made strong and authoritative by the
sanction of religion ; so strong that for centuries they
have shaped society, and resisted all hostile influences.
When, for instance, Hindu supremacy gave way to

Mahomedan domination, Aryan ideas and customs had become so fixed that they not only resisted Mahomedan proselyting zeal more successfully than any other Asiatic or African race, but have Hinduized Mahomedanism to a marked degree.

Of all people they have least sought intercourse with others, and are the most reluctant to leave their own manner of life, and adopt that of foreigners. They dread and dislike emigration, and even to leave their own province for permanent residence in another. During three thousand years there is but one feeble instance on record of any attempt on their part at conquest or colonization. That which has been handed down from past generations is accepted as sacred and immutable, and to change is to dishonour parentage, to discredit the community, and come perilously near an act of sacrilege. From these causes it has come to pass that Hindu society has developed and hardened into a form more exclusive, conservative, and immobile than is to be found in any other race. The status of women is one of its most marked manifestations, and some of the intellectual characteristics which have led to such a peculiar result are quite traceable.

Asiatic habitude of mind and sentiment is one of these conditions. Two features have always characterized Asiatics : a low estimate of women and an acquiescence in absolute rule, whether in the state or the family. Nowhere is the position of women what it should be. It varies, of course, but nowhere does it approach to that which is now the recognized ideal

of Protestant Christendom. And it is lower in India
than anywhere else. Power, not right, or truth, or
love, or justice, has always been the supreme ruler.
So absolute and unchallenged has been its sway
that it is everywhere acknowledged as conferring a
right to its arbitrary use, and is submitted to with
a patient acquiescence perplexing to Western minds.
It is an historical fact that despotism has been the
note of every monarchy throughout Asia; that a
representative government, either under the form of
a constitutional monarchy or a republic, has never
existed, or even been seriously thought of; and that
all uprisings against despotism and tyranny have
had their basis, not in popular rights or a sense of
justice, but in a crave for vengeance or a thirst to
possess power. The idea that power confers right,
that its possessor is above law, or, if there is a law,
may ignore or evade it if he can, pervades all classes.
It is as characteristic of the peasant, the policeman,
the strong man, the capitalist, and the landholder, as
of the emperor. Even where law is recognized, as
in China, and wherever the Koran is accepted as
divine, it either confers absolute authority on rulers,
or power in the practical forms of despotism, and
tyranny overrides law. This is the general drift of
things, since corruption is universal, and the people
are too ignorant, abject, and suspicious to combine
for good or useful purposes; for the oppressed would
become oppressors, and slaves despots, if fortune gave
them the opportunity. Appeals, therefore, such as

rouse men of Western race to face peril and dare danger for freedom, for justice, for the right, never have been raised in Eastern lands, and would have elicited no response if they had. This assists us to understand how and why men oppress women, and why the oppression for these long weary centuries has been so patiently endured, and why women are nowhere placed side by side as the equals of men, but behind or below them. They are physically weaker, and their intellectual and emotional qualities are, however admirable, of a nature that non-Christian men neither easily perceive nor cheerfully recognize ; so that though their beauty, grace, and delicacy of perception are freely acknowledged, they are pressed down to a subordinate, if not servile, condition in the family as well as in the state.

Suspicion and distrust are among the strongest and saddest of Asiatic characteristics, but nowhere are they more seen than in India. These have been intensified by long centuries of despotism, oppression, and wrong. Few trust even their own kindred. Women suffer the most from this for two reasons. Being the weaker and more dependent, men can exert their power over the conditions of woman's life as women cannot over men's ; hence the latter, when able, allow no freedom of thought or action to the former. Then, further, men, knowing what they and other men are, and untaught by the popular forms of religion the necessity and duty of moral restraint, become suspicious of the fidelity and moral integrity of others,

and exhibit their jealousy by restricting the liberty
of all women, whenever they have the power to do so.
An acute writer, familiar with the people, has well
said, ' To the Hindu, jealous to madness of ceremonial
purity, on which, as he conceives, the happiness of his
future life depends, and drilled by centuries of foreign
domination to suspect oppression in the very breezes
—his shrouded domestic life is all in all, the one thing
in defence of which he will die or be ruined.'   It
inevitably follows that by a process of reasoning and
feeling it is unnecessary to describe, women are
distrusted, and when practicable, guarded in a manner
suggestive of utter distrust, and which by all
European women would be regarded as alike
degrading and insulting.

Then *the inveterate caste idea* favours a low estimate
of women, and the various forms of repressive treatment to which they are liable.   Believing that each
of the four great castes were distinct creations, as
separate from one another and from non-Hindu races
as one race of animals is from another, and that intercourse and intermixture partake both of sinful and
unnatural qualities, and that degradation of birth
comes from the taint acquired in a previous form of
existence—it is easily assumed that women are not
the equals of men, and may properly, therefore, be
treated as inferiors.

If distrust and sentiment, not far apart from contempt, shapes man's policy toward them, so does
affection and a jealous concern for the integrity and

well-being of the family and the caste of which he is a member. Kindness and benevolence, indeed, influence him, strange as may seem to be the forms they assume ; and if he were charged with cruelty or heartlessness in his treatment of the female members of his family, he would indignantly repel the charge. However mistaken, he acts as their guardian and protector, and assumes he best discharges his duty by treating them as dependents, not equals, and allowing them the exercise of as little power and liberty as possible.

Women need a powerful protector and friend, and in India they have seldom had one.[1] Physically they are weak, socially they are dependent, and intellectually they are less able to combine for common aims than men. This is specially so in barbarous states of society, such as heathenism almost always exhibits. Unless, therefore, some strong power or principle of right, mercy, love, soften the hearts of men toward them, they will be thrust down and degraded, and then distrusted. That is man's way all the world over toward women—when left free and uncontrolled.

---

[1] This has been a fact all through history, but it will not remain so, and the change, wherever Christianity gains power, is evidence of its essential superiority to every other religion. No other has ever given to women the opportunity to become their better, nobler selves. The love and justice it ever teaches, the strong and settled conditions of society it establishes, the respect for women it ever cultivates in men, and the freedom it gives to women, with the culture of mind, character, and life which grow into such mingled strength, purity, and beauty where it gains power, contrasts purely Christian society with every form of heathen life. These will surely grow, and their richest development will be seen in the higher status and blessed influence of womankind all through the East.

In religion should reside that benignant, restraining power. But it has never existed in Hinduism. It has always been on the side of the strong. It has never protected the weak or protested against oppression, or striven to lift up the fallen or protect the unfortunate. It knows nothing of justice, charity, pity. Its entire drift has been to brand and degrade

A HINDU TRAINING CLASS (SOUTH INDIA).

women, and to keep them degraded. What else has it ever done for them? and yet this is one of the religions of the East we are invited to respect and admire! Christianity has done more in the past fifty years to soften and brighten the lot of Hindu women —to wipe away their tears, to break their fetters, to

give them their true place of right and charm—than
Hinduism has done in 3000 !   And herein is one of
the great glories of our sublime and divine faith ; it
holds back the strong from oppressing and wronging
the weak, and makes for women opportunities for the
exercise of their gifts and charms, which win for them
their true place by the side of men, and not behind or
below them.

Happily, this benignant power, which ever makes
for righteousness, is beginning to work, and already
there are signs of its power to cause even 'the
wilderness and solitary place to be glad, and the
desert to rejoice and blossom as the rose.'

It is usual for those who, in the present age, are
sufficiently enlightened to desire social reform, to
ascribe the subordinate and secluded condition of
women to the influence of Mahomedanism.   No
doubt it everywhere sanctions polygamy, crushes down
liberty, endangers the purity of domestic life, and
never gives women the respect and honour which
are their due.   And in India, being no better than
elsewhere, it has given abundant cause for suspicion
and dread.   But it did not introduce, though it
stimulated, the pernicious sentiments referred to.
After the dawn of Aryan history, in the Vedic age, it
is doubtful if women have ever had their true place
in society, whilst the evidence is conclusive that
some of the worst evils from which they have suffered
had a distinctly Hindu origin, and were in force long
anterior to the ages of Mahomedan domination.

CHAPTER XII.

THE history of Hinduism is very suggestive and disappointing. If it could be adequately written, it would be a record of minds unusually acute, speculative, and devout, attempting to interpret for their own satisfaction and the guidance of the multitude, the great features of nature and the deep mysteries underlying all systems of religion. And with results neither adequate nor satisfying. Such a history would be a most valuable contribution to our knowledge of comparative religions, and an extraordinary record of devoutness, intellectual subtlety, unfruitful speculation, and progress downward.

The old idea that the immobility of the East extended to the domain of speculative and practical religion has been exploded. Hinduism has been subject to modifying influences all through its history. Philosophers, priests, rulers, reformers ; powerful influences from the aboriginal tribes it absorbed ; the sects and parties which have arisen in its own bosom ;

external influence from Mahomedanism, and internal pressure from pundits on one side and the superstitious multitude on the other, have all had a formative influence in making it what now it is—the most complex, varied, and stupendous system of abstract speculation and practical superstition the world has ever seen.

And it is a most impressive evidence of the absolute need of a Divine revelation ; a convincing proof that 'the world by wisdom knows not God ;' that in the course of centuries the attempts to reform it have been so few and so ineffectual, whilst it has even tended to become more polytheistic, gross, and debased, like an animal in the quicksands, whose struggles to be free increase its weakness and danger.

It should be remembered, in justice to Hindus, that this tendency to religious deterioration is not confined to them. Wherever mankind are left without the Divine light and moral force which come from the Sacred Scriptures, a lack of power to find out God, to rise toward the good, the pure, and the true, and a greater tendency to drift downward, and to allow evil rather than to combine for the purpose of resisting and overthrowing it, is seen. Nowhere are the evidences of this more abundant than in India. It is, for instance, admitted, even by those who take the most optimistic views of the present status of Indian women, that their position in Vedic times, in the heroic ages, and even for a long subsequent time, was far higher than in the centuries nearer our own. And there is no evidence that any serious attempt was made to guard the simpler and purer usages of ancient times from changes that were alike unjust and cruel.

During the long ages that some of these usages at least have been prevalent, over populations greater than those of European kingdoms, no great popular movement, or protest even, from any class of influential leaders has been uttered against perpetual widowhood, infanticide, child marriage, female immolation, or any combined movement taken place to elevate their status or improve the hard conditions of their lot.

Happily now for Indian society generally, and for women specially, 'the night is far spent, the day is at hand.' The light of Christianity has begun to shine even where the darkness was most dense. It is being borne aloft and carried forward by a race gifted and qualified for so great an enterprise, and the evidence that they will be honoured to bring light and peace and joy to Indian homes is seen in this—that the light and love they bring are heaven-borne, and therefore have a Divine force ; that the race who bear them have evidently been called by the Divine voice and guided by the Divine hand ; and that, to the extent the remedy has been applied, it has been most efficacious.

Christianity comes to all as a revelation from God. It bears the evidences of its Divine origin in

M

the righteousness, love, goodness, and sweet reasonableness of its spirit, principles, and precepts. The evidence of this is seen in all the foreshadowings of its gracious reign ; in the utterances of Jewish seers, when surrounded by the injustice, oppression, cruelty, and vice of heathen nations ; in the perfect character and life of the Founder of our religion, the Flower of our humanity ; in the truths taught and the spirit expressed by Him and His inspired disciples ; in their adaptation to all men and all ages ; and in the actual power of this religion to combat and destroy all the evils afflicting society, as far as it is truly applied. It is sufficient evidence of this here to point out that it abolished amphitheatrical games throughout the Roman Empire, and slavery and serfdom throughout Europe ; has everywhere raised and purified the status of women ; whilst for the social evils that vex Christian lands it cannot be held responsible, since they exist in direct violation of its commands. It may be added that the present institutions and usages of Hindu feminine life could not possibly continue if Christianity prevailed ; the former would melt away as inevitably as snow in April.

Then, Christianity in India, as in every land to which it is faithfully carried, comes to change 'the wilderness into a garden,' 'to break every yoke,' 'to proclaim liberty to the captive and the opening of the prison to them that are bound.'[1] And it is prosecuting its beneficent aims under circumstances singularly

[1] Isa. lx., lxi. ; Ps. lxxii.

auspicious. Chiefly it has been brought, and certainly prosecutes its peaceful aims, under the protection of a race which, however defective otherwise, exhibits the social and domestic virtues more attractively than does any other.

This race seems to be guided to this and analogous work by a power higher than their own, that is, to be an agency designed by God, providentially to serve His purposes by greatly benefiting another and yet more numerous race.

1. That the English should be supreme in India is one of the most marvellous events in history; and the course of events leading to this, justifies the conviction that God has led us to this unique position—that in and beyond the aims of men and communities, urged onward by the mixed motives common to humanity, a Divine power has been drawing England and India alike into unique relations. That a company of merchants and adventurers, without any purpose other than making money by honest trading and without a thought of imperial supremacy, should have been led on unconsciously to lay the foundations of an empire, then only reached by a three or four months' voyage, containing one-fifth of the human race, or more than twice the population of the Roman Empire when at its zenith, is the most unique event in the history of conquest and empire. England never dreamt of such a splendid issue, but it has come, we believe, by the leadings of Divine providence. Through treaties and alliances with native states;

through conflict or competition with four European nations ; through wars more frequently forced on us or waged in self-defence than is usually supposed ; and the responsibilities of our position, constraining us to defend ourselves and the people who have come under our rule ;—we have been led on to supreme authority over this vast and varied empire.   Surely the hand of God has been in this !   As He led the Israelites into Canaan, to witness for monotheism and purity of life against the heathenism and immorality of the surrounding nations, and in a subsequent age dispersed them over the civilized world to witness for Him and to prepare the nations for the Gospel message, so now has He given to the most Protestant, free, tolerant, and morally earnest of nations, dominion over the most polytheistic and mentally and morally enthralled of all the great races of mankind.   It is not presumption, but a true and devout interpretation of events, which leads us to believe that God thus designed to give to our race a supreme opportunity to glorify Himself and to bless and elevate a vast and ancient race.

2. Defective as the British race may be, it yet has special, definite qualifications for the stupendous and glorious work needing to be accomplished.

Into the details of this interesting question we can-not enter, but confining our attention to the one great question of the emancipation of women, it may confidently be alleged that domestic life is purer in Anglo-Saxon society, and women more justly and respectfully treated, and made more the equals and companions of men, than anywhere else. Further, we have offended less against the laws of purity in our intercourse with darker races, and done far less to awaken suspicion and arouse race hatred than any other people ; than, for instance, the Portuguese, the Spaniards, the French, or even the Dutch.

Not only has there been, especially for two generations, a marked avoidance of sins against family integrity, all over British India—alas, that there should be exceptions to this rule !—but in most of our civil stations, where the people have the means of observing what manner of lives we lead, and are usually sagacious in their observations, and in the few great centres where now official Europeans reside, there are seen practical illustrations of the purity, freedom, and happiness of family life, which, though matters of course to us, are narrowly observed by the people, and impress them greatly. English women are free ; they walk and ride abroad ; they sit at the same table as men ; they mingle in public society ; they are seen with unveiled faces, and they look happy and unconstrained ; they read, they write, they bear themselves with modesty and grace, and are always treated with respect and courtesy. All this is observed, talked about, wondered at, and contrasted with native ways and all the traditions of the past.

But there is this difference between their observation of our ways and ours of theirs. They look at ours passively, with much amazement, but with little effort

to bring theirs into accord with ours, and with but a
sluggish wish, here and there, that theirs should be
abandoned for ours. Usage, rules, and example have
little force, being neutralized by the sentiment, which
whilst seeming to us expressive of indolence and
apathy is to them conclusive that nothing more is to
be said, 'Yes, that is their custom, and of course it is
proper for them ; but ours is different, and it would
be improper for us to do as they do.' Therefore the
weary yoke is borne meekly and patiently. We, on
the other hand, with our contempt for mere usage,
our eager wish for change and progress, our habit of
asking to know the reason why, our energy, our
moral indignation against any customs and usages
which seem to us unjust and cruel, especially if they
are so to the oppressed and weak, our reluctance to
stand passively by whilst others suffer, even if their
relations to ourselves are remote, our English race
qualities, sanctified and directed by the leaven of Christianity, are impelled and eager to seek by every fair,
wise, just method, the emancipation of Indian women
from all usages that to us seem wrong. We are as
the Stanley expedition, resolved to rescue and free
the Emin Pasha of Hindu womanhood, even in spite
of its own apathy and helplessness ; and, though slowly
and sluggishly, this immense stream of erroneous
thinking and feeling is giving signs of change.

    And our history in India is in this direction not
only free from reproach, but most honourable. We
have abolished suttee. We have made it penal

to bury parents alive, or to kill any one, under
the veil of religion, on the banks of sacred
rivers. We have caused to cease human sacrifices
in temples, and offerings of living boys and girls to
propitiate the earth goddess. We have brought to
an end the sacrifice of children in the Ganges, at
the great centres of pilgrimage at Allahabad, Gunga
Saugor, and elsewhere. We have prohibited infanticide throughout our empire, and greatly diminished
it in the feudatory states. We have legalized the
marriage of widows. We have initiated and encouraged every movement for the elevation of
women. We have, in all these movements, been
considerate of the usages and even prejudices of
others. We have been respectful of native suscepti-
bilities, and have never rudely or haughtily dis-
regarded them. We have used argument and
persuasion rather than force. We have usually
carried the wisest and best, and therefore the most
influential portions of society with us by the sweet
reasonableness of our polity, its unselfishness, and
its appeal to the deeper, truer springs of native
humanity. Therefore, the vast and varied changes
that are passing over Indian society are attended with
so little friction, and win for the English race confidence and respect rather than distrust and ill will.[1]

[1] All this justifies the following words, which go far to vindicate the
East India Company's government from unmerited depreciation.
' At no period in the history of the Christian Church, not even in the
brilliant century of legislation, from Constantine's Edict of Toleration

And now that the people have some knowledge
of the truths and principles of Christianity, and owe
allegiance to a race which, whatever its defects, loves
truth and justice, respects the rights of all men,
abhors cruelty and wrong, has sympathy with the
oppressed and weak, and gives to women a higher
and more rational place of respect and honour than
any other people, it is inevitable that the change
of opinion and sentiment relative to the status of
women, seen here and there, must extend and affect
all castes and classes. Various forces press in this
direction, and must finally triumph over ancient
customs and prejudices. Among these are the
monogamous customs and chivalrous sentiments of
Europeans ; the spread of enlightened opinion among
the people ; the readiness of the Government to
legislate when public opinion encourages and justifies
its action, and, above all, the Divine energy of
Christian missions. England takes the lead in this
most Christ-like of all enterprises, happily emulated
by that larger England across the sea. Few indeed
understand the grandeur and far-reaching beneficence of the missionary idea, and many, through
lack of Divine insight and want of knowledge and
sympathy with spiritual and Divine aims, fail to

to the Theodotian Code, has Christianity been the means of abolishing
so many inhuman customs and crimes, as were suppressed in India by
the Company's Regulations and Acts in the first half of the nineteenth
century.' Is not all this the pledge and presage of inevitable progress
and glorious issues in all the relations of family life ?—*The Conversion
of India*, p. 110, by Dr. George Smith.

appreciate its principles and results. They stand, nevertheless, as the highest of all attempts to express to all men the love and pity of God through the Gospel of our Lord and Saviour Jesus Christ ; and of their aims and policy in India, this may be said —in addition to their primary aim of preaching the Gospel to every creature, they have done more than any other agency, perhaps more than all others united—to guard our countrymen from irreligiousness and moral deterioration, to draw them toward Christ and true Christianity ; and to influence the Government toward a beneficent and humane policy. They have uniformly and courageously taught the great principles of truth, justice, and righteousness ; they have led the attack on every abuse and evil which have so long afflicted society ; and the new ideas about the status of women, which everywhere are springing into life and vigour, owe more to them than to any other source.

God has called the English race by imperial rule, and His Church by the beneficent and holy power of religion, to bring about one of the greatest— perhaps, indeed, the greatest—social, moral, and religious changes ever wrought in a vast empire. Would that we comprehended the grandeur of our mission, and were suitably impressed with a consciousness of our responsibility !

The relative influence of these, the methods and policies it were wisest for them to pursue, in the prosecution of their stupendous and difficult task, demand an amount of attention they never receive, and that cannot now be attempted to define. A part of this great question, cognate to our subject, may, however, here be suggested. For instance, on what lines and in what directions should the elevation of Hindu women proceed? Is our Western ideal of social and family life the true one for an Eastern race? Are there not deep differences of country and nationality, which may render it advisable for change to move in a direction of its own—somewhere, for instance, between what it and ours now are? the most advisable age for marriage? the degree of parental control in marriage? the most suitable education for a Hindu woman?—her place in the family, in the councils of her husband, and the extent of her freedom and intercourse with others, and the relative merits of collective patriarchal family life as in India, and our separative method?—these are features of importance, worthy of more consideration than they receive. This only now need be said—It is most important that all change of opinion, sentiment, and practice should be gradual, and that native opinion should precede, not only a change of usage, but all legislative action.

A CRITICISM LESSON IN TRAVANCORE.

CHRISTIAN GIRLS' SCHOOL (CALCUTTA).

CHAPTER XIII.

EFFORTS ALREADY MADE TO BENEFIT WOMEN.

THE earliest mission schools were intended for both sexes and all castes and classes; but increased knowledge and experience convinced the missionaries that prejudice was far too strong for their good intentions, and their schools were left almost entirely to boys belonging to the inferior castes. When it became known that, whilst education was greatly valued for boys, there was a deep prejudice against it

for girls, and that this was but one feature of the
degradation and unhappy condition of their sex, the
desire became strong to instruct and elevate them in
some practicable way. The construction of society
and the prejudices everywhere dominant, alike among
rich and poor, high caste and low, made this most
difficult. They could preach, but the women were
not present to listen. They conversed with men, but
few opportunities were allowed them to do so with
women. They published books and tracts, but not
one woman in 20,000 could read, even if a Christian
publication could have been placed in their hands.
It may seem strange that zenana visitation was not
thought of as a means of reaching the most secluded
and influential class of women, but a long leavening
process was necessary to make that practicable, and
far into this century even, where now it is cautiously
and suspiciously received, the force of custom, the
seclusiveness of zenana life, the distrust of the men,
the fear of the women, and the dread of intercourse
with Christians, prevented the idea from being even
entertained.

But Christian women were not indifferent, and
brooded sorrowfully over the sad state of their native
sisters. And they did what they could. *They formed
schools wherever practicable, for Eurasian and native
Christian girls*, and to these Hindus and Mahomedans were usually welcome. But, since they could
induce few to attend, they established *boarding-schools*
and *orphan asylums*, into which were received the few

children offered by their relatives, and now and then the many who were left orphans and homeless by terrible famines.

These, however, were neither satisfactory in themselves, nor did they reach any considerable part of the community. The board of each child cost little, but the general expenses of a school were considerable, and the girls and boys thus brought up seldom exhibited marked features of energy, strength of character, and self-reliance. They were for the most part exotics, not hardy plants ; nor did such schools influence, either by their character or number, the vast populations surrounding them.

Bazaar day schools, therefore, were formed in towns where missionaries resided, and common schools for girls in villages where their influence extended. In some few instances even mixed schools were formed· In 1815, the Rev. Mr. May, of the L.M.S., had about 29 schools under his charge around Chinsurah, in Bengal, in which were 3500 scholars ; and since in one of these there were 40 boys and 17 girls, it is fair to conclude that some of both sexes were received into some at least of the others. In 1820, the same society had in Madras a circle of schools in which were 'between 600 and 700 boys, beside females.' In the year following, it is reported of a section of these schools that 'the number of boys amounted to 126, and that of girls to 68.'[1]

---

[1] An attempt to advance beyond this by establishing a school for girls of a more respectable class met with no encouragement, for we

The general character of the bazaar schools exhibits
the difficulties with which missionaries had to contend.
Parents could understand that education was a
privilege, and might be a gain to boys, but for girls
it seemed to be useless, if not pernicious. Female
education had evil associations, for were not harlots
more generally trained than any other women? The
superstition was general that educated women made
disobedient wives, and that the husbands of girls who
could read were most liable to die. Education, it
was everywhere assumed, would cause girls to be

read in the report for 1822, 'There exists no immediate prospect of
establishing the projected female school, as the national prejudice
against the education of females continues to prevail in its full vigour.'
And a year or two later, referring to the same design, 'The repugnance
which is felt by the natives generally to female education imposes a
serious impediment to this branch of the mission.'

In Bombay Mrs. Wilson had to contend with similar difficulties, but
met with more success. She and Dr. Wilson reached India early in
1829, and before the end of the year both of them were conversant with
the Maraithi language. 'She visited native women, induced them to
send their daughters to a school she had organized, and before three
months had expired she had 53 scholars, and before she had been
double that time in Bombay, there were six schools with 120 scholars.'
She then founded a home for poor and destitute girls, into which 23
were received.

'In about three years, 126 girls attended the mission classes, and
much good work was in progress, though hindrances were many and
wearying.'

This noble woman died, after a brief but remarkably useful life, in
1835. A sentence from one of her letters suggests where true honour
and happiness are seldom sought, but often found : 'Had I contem-
plated at a distance the number and variety of duties which now
devolve upon me, I should have been appalled at the prospect,
but, instead of lessening, they add greatly to my enjoyment.' The
results of her labours still live.

conceited and unmanageable. Since purdah ladies were untaught, what presumption was it for the poor and low caste to learn to read and write! Nothing but evil and danger could spring out of such an unheard-of revolution! Think of the trouble and danger it would cause! How could girls, however low in caste and poor, go to school unwatched and untended! It would interfere with their meals, their devotions, their freedom, and endanger their caste, if not their lives! Such were the difficulties suggested by ignorant and superstitious parents, in whose wide circle of relationship no reader probably could be discovered for generations.

To meet these objections, many expedients were adopted. A woman was sent round to conduct the girls to school and home again, who was stimulated to zeal by payment for as many as were brought. Often the scholars were paid for attendance. Usually food or sweetmeats were provided for them, and periodically they received, even for meagre attendance, gifts of money or presents of cloth. Each sum was small, but the aggregate amount was considerable. The results were far from encouraging. The attendance was most irregular. It ceased altogether for trivial or imaginary causes. A desire to learn was seldom seen on the part of scholars or parents, but greed and suspicion were ever on the alert to have discipline and rule relaxed, or to obtain additional gifts. Now and then the school would be entirely deserted through some foolish or evil report. An

N

attendance of twenty-five girls was regarded as encouraging. They almost always came from the lowest castes and classes, and left before they were eleven years of age, to be married, or on some trivial pretence or other. Thus, through their early age, the superficiality of their knowledge, and the dense ignorance of all their surroundings, they retained little of what they had learned, which usually soon disappeared as raindrops in the rushing river.

These schools, however, though few and small, were *educational* in a wide and general sense. They were in every instance the outcome of the zeal and love of missionaries' wives and their friends. They drew the attention of the high and low castes alike to Christianity and its principles. They exhibited the mindful, disinterested zeal of the missionaries for the poor, the ignorant, and the despised. They conveyed some knowledge of Christian truth and doctrine, and the ability to read and write to a few in various towns in many Indian provinces. They helped to familiarize the people with missionary methods, and some aspects of European life and policy, and they assisted to make Christian people more conscious of the degradation and dense ignorance of Hindu women, and the peculiar difficulties to be encountered in reaching them.

There was much searching of heart and a large expenditure of love and pity as well as of much time and money, on the part of individual missionaries and their wives, before as well as after concerted and

combined action was taken to improve on these imperfect and even doubtful methods ; for be it observed
the missionaries—the only class who cared practically
for the education of women—were by no means
satisfied with what they were doing. They desired
to do more, to reach a much wider circle. But custom,
prejudice, and the strange immobility of native society
barred their way, as a vast wall of ice the southward
progress of the antarctic voyager.

A glance at the general state of education early
in this century may now be given. There had always
been a strong appreciation of education among the
people. Colleges for the training of Brahmins in
Sanscrit lore existed here and there, and were held
in high repute. But all over India primitive
elementary schools for boys were valued.

Early in the century the Indian Government saw
the importance of encouraging education, and in
a crude, tentative manner did so on a limited scale.
Colleges were established at Benares and Calcutta
in 1781 and 1791, on a purely vernacular basis, and
one of much importance on a broader basis in
Calcutta in 1816. But an important step was taken
in 1823, when the Government resolved on the
formation of a ' General Committee of Public Instruction, for the purpose of ascertaining the state of
public education, for the introduction of useful knowledge, and for the encouragement of native literature.'
The Council was formed, but for twelve years the
policy to be adopted was the subject of warm and

even bitter controversy. It was composed of able men and enthusiastic educationalists like Lord Macaulay and Sir Charles Trevelyan, but whether the policy of the Government should be Oriental or Anglican, with various side issues, was only settled in 1835, when it was decided 'that the great object of the British Government ought to be the promotion of European literature and science among the natives of India.' There was need indeed of education, for a thorough official inquiry made in 1835—the first of the kind—led to a report that only two and a half per cent. of the great province of Bengal could read and write, and that the proportion for all India was 1 in 400.

A great advance was made in popular education in 1844, when Mr. Thomason, Governor of the North-West Provinces, adopted the policy of basing all schemes of popular education on existing native institutions. This, with modifications, was adopted by the other provincial governments, and was finally embodied in the celebrated educational despatch of Lord Dalhousie in 1854. But in that year the Government educational institutions contained only 12,000 pupils, though they rapidly increased to more than 180,000 in 1859. But none of these schools were for girls, nor was it until after the middle of the century that any recognition was made by the Government of the importance of female education. Meanwhile, the missionary party, with much earnestness, but scanty resources, sustained their schools, urged the

GIRLS' SCHOOL IN NORTH INDIA.

importance of female education, and initiated the first
combined movement in this direction.

To trace this we must return as far back as the
second decade of the century. The honour of
advancing beyond individual efforts in small separate
schools for united action, and to secure higher
efficiency in teachers and teaching, is claimed by
Dr. Duff for some young ladies associated with the
Baptist Missionary Society in Calcutta.

In April, 1819, an address was issued setting forth
the actual condition of women in Bengal, and pro-
posing the formation of a school for the education
of Hindu women. This led to the formation of an
association under the title of the *Calcutta Female
Juvenile Society, for the Education of Native Females.*
But for nearly twelve months, notwithstanding the
most strenuous exertions, the number of scholars did
not exceed eight. Still the promoters of the scheme
went on. At the end of two years the number
amounted to 32, and in three more years the schools
had increased to six, in which were 160 scholars. 'On
December 14, 1823, was held the anniversary of the
society. And that must ever prove a memorable
day in the history of feminine native education, as
it was the first time that the establishment of native·
female schools of any description could be spoken
of as in the remotest degree practicable, without
opening the windows of incredulity and drawing down
showers of ridicule and contemptuous scorn.'[1]

[1] Dr. Duff in the *Indian Female Evangelist*, vol. i. p. 59.

But though this was the first combined effort in behalf of female education, it was symptomatic of a deepening interest, and was overshadowed by another society destined to accomplish great and unexpected results. In September, 1819, *The Calcutta School Society* was founded under influential auspices, and was intended to unite Europeans and natives in a combined movement. Its leading design was 'to assist and improve schools, organized and supported by the natives themselves ; to establish new schools ; to improve the general system of education ; and to diffuse useful knowledge of every description among the inhabitants of India, but especially within the province of Bengal.' In the course of inquiry previous to active operations, it was ascertained that in the district around Calcutta, containing at least 750,000 people, there were only 4180 children in the native schools, and that with scarcely an exception Hindu girls were wholly uneducated. Further investigation brought out the appalling truth that for the entire mass of the female population there was no system of education whatever, and that out of forty million females then supposed to be in British India, probably not 400, or one in 100,000, could read or write, and of these the greater number had been educated by the wives of missionaries.[1]

[1] *The Indian Female Evangelist*, vol. i. p. 16. The society received considerable aid from missionaries. In the report of the L.M.S. for 1821, we read, 'It is well known that the Calcutta School Society is vigorously employed in the establishment and support of schools. The directors are happy to state that the operations of the society are

The society had influential friends, and acted with vigour. It applied to the British and Foreign School Society 'to select and send from England a well-qualified lady to institute schools for native girls.' Even then, however, the first idea was not so much to begin with schools, but to 'institute and superintend a school for training native female teachers, who should be selected from the daughters of our countrymen in India already acquainted with the native languages, in order that, after proper instruction, they might be fixed as schoolmistresses in suitable stations.' The first result of this movement was very remarkable, though it was not what had been arranged for. The British and Foreign School Society issued a circular, setting forth the claims of Indian women, and asking for aid that a suitable agent might be sent out. Miss Cook fortunately was selected, and reached Calcutta at the end of 1821. The issue proved that no more suitable agent could have been found, for she won for native female education an interest and enthusiasm of the highest value ; and as a system and a recognized department of missionary education of the highest importance, it dates from that time.

likely to prove of the greatest importance, and have interested them-selves very warmly in behalf of the native female population of that country, with a view to extend to them the advantages of education.' 'With a view to promote a design so closely connected with the ultimate success of missionary operations in Hindustan, the directors have committed to the disposal of Mr. Townley, one of its missionaries, the sum of £125, to be appropriated as he shall deem proper, toward the encouragement of native female education in India.'

A significant difficulty had to be overcome at the very commencement of her labours. To interest natives in the work of the School Society, it was stipulated that its managing committee should consist of two-thirds Europeans and their descendants, and one-third natives of India. But it soon appeared that the latter had no desire to engage in any general plan for female education.[1] On this the Corresponding Committee of the Church Missionary Society undertook to promote the special purposes of Miss Cook's mission. Thus her labours for many years were conducted under the auspices of that society.

A touching incident, however, led Miss Cook to establish her first girls' school much sooner than was anticipated. Two months after her arrival, when

---

[1] 'In the case of male education, the natives themselves have always been ready to co-operate with us. Nay, they have eagerly seconded our efforts, and their own indigenous institutions have furnished a common standpoint for concerted action. The same men who would have wasted their powers in elaborating ingenious word-puzzles in Sanskrit verse or in trying to comprehend incomprehensible abstractions of Sanskrit philosophy, have devoted themselves to the acquisition of scientific truth through the medium of English. But in the case of female education all the conditions have been reversed. No basis of common action has been found, no ground has been cleared, no open door has invited us to enter. Every avenue of approach has been barred and barricaded. The natives have been more than content to leave their women engulfed in the depths of profound ignorance. They have opposed every attempt at raising or enlightening them as an offence against religion and morality. Without doubt any scheme of direct Government interference for the education of Indian women would have threatened the people with vast social changes. It would have contravened the sacred usages of the most obstinately conservative nation in the world' (*Modern India*, p. 331. By Sir M.M. Williams).

learning Bengali, she paid a visit to one of the School
Society's boys' schools, with no other thought than to
learn the true pronunciation of the language. The
presence of an English lady in that part of the native
town drew a crowd around the school-door, and in
the crowd was an eager, interesting little girl, evidently
well known to the head-teacher, though he drove her
away. Miss Cook observed the incident, and on
inquiry was told that for three months the child had
come daily, begging to be allowed to learn to read
with the boys. When called and questioned, she
expressed her eagerness to learn, and Miss Cook was
informed that many more were anxious to learn, and
that she could have twenty scholars next day. On
the following morning she went, accompanied by a
lady who spoke Bengali fluently. Thirteen girls came,
and with them several women drawn by curiosity,
and to them were the intentions of Miss Cook fully
explained, apparently to the great satisfaction of the
women. But when two days afterward she went, only
seven pupils appeared, and several women as spectators, who asked suspiciously, ' What will be the use
of learning to our female children ? What advantage
will it be to them ? And what benefit will *you* derive
from it ? We suppose this is a holy work in your
eyes, and will be pleasing to God. Our husbands now
look upon us as little better than brutes.' Within a
month, two other schools were established, containing altogether between fifty and sixty girls. The
success seemed so great that the Church Missionary

Society Committee issued a circular, asking for
additional aid, and the response from persons of
distinction, headed by the Governor-General, Lord
Hastings and his lady, was such that by the end of
the year 1823 the number of schools had increased
to twenty-two, and of scholars to between three and
four hundred.   All this was accomplished in spite of
many hindrances.   Most parents were indifferent, not
a few were hostile, and all were suspicious and appre-
hensive that some dark and selfish plot on the part
of the Government was being hatched !   Some parents
went daily to see that nothing wrong was going on.
They could   not   understand   how   any   human
beings could be so disinterested as to labour and
spend money without any profitable return.   'Who
knows,' they said, 'but they will by-and-by take
away all the children?'   One teacher was so impor-
tuned that he had to sign a written document, 'that
they should take and hang him if any such thing as
they dreaded should ever happen.'

The constitution and management of these schools
had some of the defects we have already indicated as
belonging to bazaar schools.   It was difficult to obtain
suitable schoolrooms in suitable localities, and yet
more so to obtain teachers who were moderately competent, or adequate to supervise their work or to
give any solid Christian instruction.   To remedy as
far as practicable these defects, and to give the work
'a more prominent and imposing attitude,' a *Ladies'
Society for Native Female Education in Calcutta and the*

A HINDU CHRISTIAN FAMILY.

Vicinity was formed, and at the fourth public
examination of the schools, at the close of 1828, the
number of schools was thirty, and the average daily
attendance four hundred. It was deemed advisable
to improve and consolidate the work by the erection
of a central school and dwelling-house for the
European lady-superintendent, as a convenient and
efficient centre for a training and model school, and
the more efficient supervision of schools in the city
and its suburbs. This was completed at considerable cost, and became for some years the centre of
Miss Cook's—now Mrs. Wilson's—labours, where
daily from two to three hundred girls were more
efficiently taught ; the former schools being gradually
improved or abandoned.

The influence of this movement was great. It
encouraged the formation of new schools, and
suggested improvements in those already existing ;
and in the course of a few years every mission in
Calcutta, and not a few elsewhere in Bengal, had one
or more girls' schools. The good results indeed
extended to Southern India, and yet more to Bombay.[1]

---

[1] In the latter city, the wife of Dr. Wilson did much to awaken an
interest in girls' schools, where the small but influential Parsee
community adopted the idea with an enthusiasm nowhere else seen.
But the following resolutions passed by Brahmins in Bombay on
September 14, 1843, and intended to influence all castes and both
sexes, is illustrative of the deep-seated hostility with which a Christian
education was regarded generally by the sacerdotal class all over India
until recently :—

‘ 1. No Brahmin shall ever attend the school of the Christian
missionaries to learn their religion or to hear their instruction, nor

Such schools accomplished a large amount of good, and for a long time seemed all that was practicable. But they were comparatively few in number, greatly restricted in influence, and did not attract any pupils from the leading or secondary classes of Hindu society. Even as far down as 1840, when Mrs. Wilson was asked, 'What may be the number of females in Bengal actually now under instruction?' her reply was, 'I know only of about 500 girls.' And of that relatively small number, one-half at least were in her own schools. But preparations were being made in many directions for an advance.

The societies already formed were active. The Society for the Promotion of Education in the East had been formed in London in 1834, and gave generous aid and sympathy to many mission stations. This was followed, in 1838, by the Scottish Ladies' Association for the Advancement of Female Education in India, which subsequently, in 1843, the year of the disruption of the Scotch Church, became two, both of them having a distinguished history. Nor were the Missionary Societies inactive, though they had no separate organizations for female education. Even natives now began to be interested in the question, though it was much more in a theoretical than practical manner. A few Hindus of rank, observant

shall they allow their children, or any under them, to attend their schools.

' 2. All Brahmins must follow the above rule, and whoever does not follow it must be regarded an outcaste.'

of English society, and among the first to be powerfully affected by an English education, saw some of
the evils afflicting native life, had some glimpses of
a possible remedy, but were, with the rarest exceptions, too weak to apply it, or were restrained by the
hostile prejudices and usages prevalent. Here and
there, however, was one who sympathized with the
new movement, privately himself instructed his wife,
or for a time engaged the services of a daily
governess, until feminine pertinacity or social opposition closed the door. But no school for respectable
or high caste girls existed anywhere, nor indeed ever
seems to have existed, though it is stated, that what
appears a school for girls is sculptured on the rock
caves of Ajunta. Neither for some years before and
after the writer's arrival in India, in 1848, was there
a single zenana in Calcutta open to any lady
missionary. But two ideas became clear to the
missionaries, and it was in their sphere of influence
only that, up to the middle of the century, any
practical steps were taken to educate Hindu women.
The first was that the education of the men must
precede the education of the women ; the other, that
women of the higher castes could not be reached by
schools, but by family or house to house instruction.[1]

---

[1] 'From the unnatural constitution of Hindu society, the education
of females in a national point of view cannot possibly precede, cannot
even be cotemporaneous with, the education of males ; a generation of
educated males, educated, that is, after the European model, must be
the precursor of a generation of educated females.'—Dr. Duff in 1837.
  'I do not think the respectable classes will at present suffer their

But though these ideas were seething in some
minds, it was Dr. Thomas Smith who first gave
voice and form to the latter idea. In a powerful
article in the *Calcutta Christian Observer* for 1840,
on Hindu Female Education, he declared, ' If it be
impossible to get the daughters of the higher classes
to attend schools, then we must teach them without
requiring their attendance at school. If the men of
India will not permit their female relations to come
to *us* for instruction, we must send our teachers to
them.' ' If a society such as the Scottish Ladies'
Association would send out several well-qualified
female teachers, who should offer gratuitous instruction to females in their own houses, they would very
soon have their hands full. And in a few years the
cause would by that means so gain respectability
that the middle and lower classes would, with tenfold
avidity, seek after instruction in schools.' ' As a
beginning, if three well-qualified female teachers
were sent out, they might undertake the instruction of eight or ten families, privately, and at the

females to attend any public school. Even if any solitary individual
may desire to do so, the tone of society which would pronounce his
conduct to be *ungenteel*, if not impious, is likely to deter him. . . . The
custom of secluding females must undoubtedly prove an obstacle to
public female education, inasmuch as no Hindu can suffer his wife or
grown-up daughter to be seen by any person without incurring the
displeasure of the fraternity, and entailing much odium on himself. . . .
I conceive there will be no difficulty in persuading many natives to
accept the blessings of education for their women when these shall be
offered within their own doors.'—Rev. Krishna Mohan Banerjea, in
the *Calcutta Christian Observer* for 1840, p. 127.

same time conduct, with native assistance, a public school.'[1]

It will seem surprising to those unacquainted with the state of Hindu society in the middle of the century, but less so to those who are, that these suggestions took no practical form for some time, though the general question of female education engaged the attention of many minds. But it was not until the beginning of 1855 that zenana teaching on any well-conceived and definite form began by arrangements made by the Rev. J. and Mrs. Fordyce. This delay is easily explained. It was caused by the intense reluctance of Hindus, even when educated, to set aside the seclusion of the zenana by the admission of Englishwomen, however educated and refined ; and of Europeans, who were so wedded to the school system, and so impressed with the difficulty of reaching zenana ladies, that it was only after much delay and abortive efforts in the school direction that a more excellent way was adopted. But the leavening process went on, now and then illustrated by some well-meant but imperfect experiment. The superior English education given daily in Calcutta to some thousands of young men in Government and Missionary institutions, almost all of them belonging to the upper classes of society, was even before the middle of the century producing a great change of sentiment on all questions relating to feminine life and customs ; and no questions were more debated in native newspapers

---

[1] *Calcutta Christian Observer* for 1840, p. 125.

and literary gatherings. This, however, led to little
beyond talk, until a most important but cautious
movement was made by the Honourable Drinkwater
Bethune, who in 1849 established a *Native Female
School in Calcutta,* for ladies of the highest rank, and
in the following year spent £6000 in providing for
it a suitable building—a larger sum probably than
had been spent from the beginning of the century on
all the buildings erected for female education in every
form through India. Mr. Bethune's high position as a
member of Government, his remarkable zeal and
liberality, and the precautions taken to disarm native
fear and prejudice, and to secure the active co-opera-
tion of native gentlemen of the highest influence, all
favoured his most benevolent and disinterested endeavours. But they had to contend with the most
deep-seated prejudices, and the silent though powerful
hostility of almost all the heads of families, and therefore met with no success adequate to the great cost.
The issues, nevertheless, were important, though they
were indirect rather than immediate. An imperfect
education, from which Christianity was carefully
excluded, was given to many young ladies belonging
to the most influential families in Calcutta ; attention
was drawn to the question of female education in all
its forms ; the sympathy of the leading European
Government classes with the general movement stood
revealed—a most important step—and something was
done to break down intense prejudice and disarm
fear. But the school never accomplished the great

hopes of its founder and his friends, in spite of their great social influence, and the pains taken, even to the sacrifice of cherished principles, to conciliate native prejudice.

The example, and probably also the defects of Mr. Bethune's school led Dr. Duff to establish, in 1857,.a school for high-caste girls. Notwithstanding his intense convictions of what education would accomplish for the overthrow of Hinduism, he was slow to realize that the time had come for an attempt at least to give to the upper class of girls what with such splendid energy he had given to boys. But the interest taken in the Bethune school, with its limitations and defects—its attempts to reach a class shut in by brazen bolts and bars, and its obsequiousness to some of the worst features of Hindu prejudice, and, above all, its careful exclusion of all Christian teaching, stirred his intense evangelical ardour, and he founded a school which in theory combined the praiseworthy aims of the former with a rigid exclusion of its defects. It was a brave and noble attempt, and it has done much good for many years ; but few benevolent and religious attempts in India are what in English estimation would be called brilliant successes ; for Indian sentiment and usage change most slowly and resist impression, as granite rocks resist the air and dew and rain.

We now return from the record of personal efforts such as those of Mr. Bethune and Dr. Duff—for the latter was complementary to the former—to narrate in chronological order the various steps by which the education of women has so far been made practicable.

A most important step in advance was the formation in 1851 of the *Normal School for the Training of Christian Female Teachers*. As schools increased in number, the need of more trained and competent teachers began to be severely felt. Missionaries' wives and daughters did noble, disinterested service, as indeed they had ever done. They engaged, superintended, and not infrequently paid for, the services of Eurasian and native women, who for the most part had little zeal and less qualification for the teacher's office. The only trained teachers were the few sent by the Missionary Societies or the Society for the Promotion of Female Education in the East, which then stood almost alone, unobtrusively doing a great work, which should be held in grateful remembrance. There was urgent need, therefore, for some influential organization to supply competent teachers for schools and private visitation. The Normal School was founded for the purpose, and its history affords ample proof of its great efficiency and success. Mrs. Wilson's Central School had for some time made this a part of its aim, and in 1857 the two institutions were united under the title of Normal, Central, and Branch Schools, and ever since have rendered invaluable service to the cause of female education.

A great demand had happily arisen for respectable and well-trained teachers, through an event which merits more than a passing notice, for it marks the commencement of organized zenana instruction, one of the most important and successful of the agencies revolutionizing the position of the many tens of million women in India. In January, 1853, the Rev. John Fordyce arrived in Calcutta to superintend the Free Church Female Institution, and intercourse with Dr. Smith and his own sagacious observation soon convinced him that zenana visitation was the true way to reach the higher classes, and make female education effective and popular. But the difficulties were great and peculiar. Even when the idea of Mr. Fordyce and Dr. Smith was considered by the Calcutta Missionary Conference, nearly all the members, many of them men of wide experience, accounted the idea to be impracticable; nevertheless Mr. Fordyce persevered, greatly aided by the wide influence among native gentlemen of Dr. Smith. He lectured on 'The Emancipation of Women in India;' wrote 'Fly-leaves for Indian Homes;' visited native gentlemen, that he might overcome their scruples, learn their objections, and gain their support; collected subscriptions, advanced the necessary funds, organized a small staff of teachers; obtained permission for them to visit regularly some families, and the promise of payment for instruction given. Mr. Fordyce writes, 'As Miss Toogood and Rebecca, the native teacher, left the house to begin these visitations, I said to Mrs. Fordyce, " This is the beginning of a new era for India's daughters." It had been a subject of much thought, consultation, and prayer, and we expected great results, but the rapidity of the extension had gone beyond our expectation. We had no opposition, but few encouraged us, and many thought that we were attempting impossibilities.' [1]

The enterprise so happily begun went on and prospered. 'As the experiment was successful, friends of the mission multiplied,' and in September, 1855, when Mr. Fordyce read a paper on Female Education before the Bengal Missionary Conference, in which the results of his work for some months were recorded, the following resolution was passed : ' They rejoice in the hopeful commencement of the Zenana School scheme, both as a sign of progress and a new means for the elevation of women in India.'

We have here given the true history of the zenana movement, since its origin has been ascribed to at least four persons. A vague idea of some such method was no doubt brooding in many minds. The native gentlemen who thought on the subject knew that family instruction alone would be feasible; but they were silent. In the few instances where instruction was desired, it was obtained through the services of a daily governess. A few English ladies, as Mrs. Tracey in Benares, Miss Bird at Goruckpore and Calcutta, Mrs. Sale in Eastern Bengal, Mrs. Mullens in Calcutta, and probably others, were zealous for female education, and had given instruction, each probably in two or

---

[1] *Women's Work in Heathen Lands: After many Days*, by the Rev. John Fordyce, late of Calcutta and Simla.

more zenanas prior to 1853.[1] From personal knowledge, the writer can state how zealously and efficiently
Mrs. Mullens did this from about 1850 to the time
of her death. But the honour of erecting zenana
teaching into a system, and of popularizing it by
public advocacy and efficient practical organization,
belongs to Mr. Fordyce and Dr. Thomas Smith, the
latter being the original advocate of the idea in 1840,
and the most zealous helper of Mr. Fordyce.

How female education has advanced in late years,
after its long struggle with opposing influences, may
be briefly stated for the glory of God, the honour
of Christian ladies, and a fine illustration of the
power of Christian beneficence to triumph over
difficulties and to confer blessings.

According to Dr. Duff, as far as the second decade
of the century, 'female education of any kind did
not exist in India at all. And not only so, but any
attempt to initiate it was resented as absolutely
impracticable.' There were a small number of indigenous schools, but from these, 'with scarcely any
exception, girls were wholly excluded.' In 1840, as
we have seen, Mrs. Wilson stated that she did not
know of more than 500 girls at school in all Bengal.
Even in 1855, the number of girls being taught was
not more than 1000 or 1200, in a population of 20
millions ; and in the presidencies of Madras and
Bombay, it being assumed that a somewhat larger

---

[1] See *Women's Work in Heathen Lands: After many Days,* by the
Rev. John Fordyce. Published by Menzies & Co, Edinburgh.

number were at school, 'there would only be 5000 or 6000 females under tuition in a total Indian female population of from 80 to 100 millions, or one girl out of about 15,000 females.'[1]

Until the middle of the century, female education had been left entirely to missionary and private effort ; but, in 1849, Lord Dalhousie, the greatest of the Governor-Generals, excepting Warren Hastings, 'on his own responsibility,' committed the Government to what he termed the 'frank and cordial support of native female education.' 'He gave grants of public money to girls' schools, and bestowed public honours on native gentlemen who established such schools, and all that he was free to do, apart from legal authority, he encouraged by his vast influence and example.' But it was not until the issue of the great educational despatch of 1854 that the Government declared itself in favour of female education, and even after for some years, languidly, if not timidly, gave practical effect to its public declaration.

The earliest and most detailed report of the progress of Christian female education was made by Dr. Mullens in 1851, and again in 1861 :—

	1851.		1861.
Day Schools ...	285	...	261
Pupils	8919	...	12,057
Boarding Schools ...	86		108
Pupils	2274	... ...	3912

---

[1] Paper read before the General Conference of Bengal Missionaries in December, 1855, by the Rev. J. Fordyce.

At the latter date, Government schools were 71, with 2545 scholars.

From this time education in all its forms has spread, but most markedly in zenanas, among the upper classes of society, though the immense numbers yet without any instruction seems to dwarf what progress already is made. For instance, in 1870-71, out of 26 million boys and girls who ought to have been at school, only 1,100,000 received any education worthy of the name, and of these only 50,000 were girls ; 22,000 being in schools belonging to Government. The rest were cared for chiefly by Christian missionaries, with the aid of small grants.[1]

The following table, from the Census Report of 1891, gives a general summary of the educational state of nine-tenths of India :—

	Total.		Males.	Females.
Learning ...	3,195,220	...	2,997,558	197,662
Literate ...	12,097,530	...	11,554,035	543,495
Illiterate ...	246,546,176	...	118,819,408	127,726,768
Total ...	261,838,926	...	133,371,001	128,467,925

Here is abundant food for reflection. It is pleasant to observe that the number of readers has now reached twelve millions, but only one in 22 are girls ; whilst of all females only six in every thousand are in any sense literate.

It is to the honour of the Missionary Societies that they have been, in every instance, the pioneers of

---

[1] 'Government Education in India,' by Dr. George Smith, in the *Female Evangelist* for April, 1872.

female education and its most active workers in every
department ; and in no sphere of evangelistic effort
have they advanced more rapidly, as the following
tables will show :—

	1871.		1890.
Foreign and Eurasian Agents	370	...	711
Native Christian	837	... ...	3278
Non-Christian	—	... ...	383
Day Schools ...	664	... ...	1507
Scholars ...	24,078	... ...	62,414
Orphans ...	2905	...	1784
Zenanas	1300	... ...	40,513 [1]

Satisfactory as these numbers are, they leave much
untold. For instance, non-Christian teachers were
employed before 1890, for often no others were to be
had.

The zenanas represent a much larger number of

[1] Statistical Tables of Protestant Missions in India for 1890. It
is important to call attention to the great need of elementary education
for the masses, since there is danger that the interest in zenana missions
may cause them to be unduly neglected. The education of a zenana
lady is far more important than that of a ryot's child, for it may carry
with it far-reaching issues. But zenana ladies are the tens in the great
mass of the population, the others are the millions. If, happily, a
desire for education is spreading among the former, it is also spreading
among the latter as rapidly. Any given sum of money will educate
several times as many daughters of the people as zenana ladies. Wise
economy in the use of mission funds, so as to do the most good with
the least expenditure, is of prime importance. Common day schools,
open to all girls, in which simply reading and writing with the
elementary truths of religion are taught by native women—a circle of
such schools being in charge of a competent native woman, where such
can be found, all being under missionary supervision—are of much
importance.

Such are everywhere needed. They cost little, and they may be
made of great use as an evangelizing agency.

persons than of houses. It is a low estimate to suppose that two in each family are pupils, and that double the number listen to what the visitor reads or talks of.

The figures take note of education, but not of the beneficent and evangelistic agencies, which cannot adequately be tabulated. Zenana visitation is now largely developed in these directions.

Bible-women are now largely employed, and find free access to poor and low-caste houses.

So do ladies who more directly preach and teach in village missions. Nor should we fail to take note of the relief which now reaches the sick and suffering through hospitals, dispensaries, and even house-to-house visitation.

LACE WORKERS (NAGERCOIL).

SOME LITTLE PATIENTS.

(From an electro supplied by the Zenana Bible and Medical Mission.)

CHAPTER XIV.

THE VARIOUS FORMS OF FEMALE AGENCY.

AGENCIES for the elevation of women have come into use, as increased knowledge on the part of Europeans and the removal of hindrances on the part of natives made them practicable. That now can be done which formerly was hardly possible, and which, if attempted, was regarded as extravagant and utopian.

All through the weary past, there were missionaries'
wives who had a wider and nobler ideal than they
could ever realize. If they did not dream of advancing
as far as now we venture, they certainly longed to
carry woman's training farther, and to lift it higher
than they actually found practicable. They were
held back by prejudices and usages intensely strong
and almost universally prevalent. Let no one despise
their day of small things, for they laboured nobly,
though it was cultivating a sterile soil in an ungenial
climate, for if they had not sown in tears, their sisters
would not now be reaping in joy. This needs to be
said in vindication of missionary consistency, and as
a proof of missionary persistence and triumph over
immense social obstacles. The early labourers did
the little they could do, but persistently pressed on
to do more. As soon as they had gained entrance
to one door they pressed on to another, desiring to
impart to all women the blessings of the gospel of
the grace of God, and to put it within their power to
obtain earthly as well as heavenly good.

Until far in the present century, lady missionaries
can hardly have been said to exist as a class. There
were literally no spheres open to them. The
missionaries' wives and daughters superintended the
few small day schools that struggled for existence
and the boarding-schools, with the assistance of native
Christian women. The first advance in these arose
from the formation of superior boarding-schools in
the Presidency cities, usually under the care of a

well-qualified superintendent. These were in some instances the spheres for training Eurasians and natives for such schools as were then in existence. Gradually, however, under the peaceful revolution[1] passing over Indian society through vernacular schools for the lower classes, English ones for the higher, the example of Europeans, and the leavening power of native female education, the former agencies have not only formed immensely widening spheres, but new ones have opened to an extent formerly undreamt of.

It is important to consider how these remedial agencies have been extended and modified, and to take some account of their relative value.

Bazaar schools have greatly multiplied. For a long time the missionary laboured in this vast but unpromising field alone, but since 1854 the Government has established many common schools for girls, and encouraged missionary societies and the people to

---

[1] 'Of course, much is done by other than missionary agency. Anything that tends to break up old beliefs, aids, in its degree, the reception of a new creed. In this point of view, almost everything we do in India is more or less missionary work. Not only railways and printing-presses, education, commerce, and the electric telegraph, our impartial codes, and uniform systems of administration; but our misfortunes and our mistakes, our wars, our famines, and our mutinies.

'It is, in truth, a perception of this fact which blinds many observers to the extent and character of the change which is taking place in matters of belief; everything in India is in a state of revolution. Happily for mankind, it is as yet peaceable, generally silent, and often almost unnoticed; but still it is revolution—more general, more complete, and more rapid than that which is going on in Europe' (*Indian Missions*, by Sir Bartle Frere). This was written in 1874. The intervening time has been one continued illustration of its truth.

form such schools by liberal supplementary grants. Landholders, village communities, and missionaries, as well as the Government, now establish them. In most no Christian instruction is given, and generally parental apathy, irregular attendance, and the early age at which the children leave, greatly interfere with efficiency. On the other hand, native prejudices and customs must be considered. Such schools may be sustained at little cost. They encourage order, discipline, and intelligence ; they impart the magic gift of reading and writing ; they are unfriendly to idolatry and all its sentiments and usages ; and in mission schools the Christian knowledge given, though small, is important, and often in after-life is a preparation for higher progress—when the gospel is heard or sorrow comes—revives and leads to God, and widows in their loneliness have turned their early and it may be long-neglected gift to good account as teachers. One of the earliest and most helpful of native women to Mrs. Mullens was of this class.

Here and there, in large cities, *day schools* of a higher order for the middle classes of society have been established ; but they are neither numerous nor popular, nor can be until the sentiments rooted in Hinduism are destroyed. The middle classes who attend such schools in England are in India very small, though under British rule they are rapidly growing ; but the indifference of even these classes to female education, their servile habit of imitating the social usages of those above them, and therefore encouraging early marriage and female isolation; the lack of the power of imitation on the part of the people, produced by centuries of almost unchallenged caste domination; and the small number of middle-class Christians found in any one place, and their habit of expecting things to be done for them which they should do for themselves,—have all checked the increase of such schools; but their social as well as economic and intellectual value should cause them to be encouraged wherever practicable.

Boarding-schools have not greatly advanced in number, but have been modified in character.

They now contain more native Christian girls, and fewer orphan waifs and strays. Opinion as to their value is divided. Whilst it is obvious that, as a duty and an example, Christian girls should be educated, it is objected that the education given often Euro-peanizes girls, and is such as unfits them for the future humble stations in life they are likely to occupy. Such schools often foster on the part of girls and their parents habits of the obsequiousness and dependence on mission funds, and those thus brought up seldom possess much energy or vigour of character. Such schools, moreover, are more expensive than they appear to be. Food and clothing cost little, but the aggregate amount for years of training is considerable, and the cost for agency is usually much more so.

Most native Christians are small farmers, living in quiet villages, in primitive style, and on incomes of astonishing minuteness; the women working with no small skill and industry as well as the men. To take girls too far away from such surroundings into houses, and to food and habitudes very different from those of the class out of which they come, and to which most of them must return, is alike an error in policy and finance. Great firmness is therefore necessary to secure the good such schools may produce, and to guard against the defects they are liable to suffer from.

The *remarkable increase* of zenana visitation has been pointed out, but its popularity has led to various modifications, or improvements they may properly be called. Formerly, zenana ladies were supplicants for admission, and the few natives who were willing to receive them, astutely knowing that they were conferring a favour as well as receiving a benefit, stipulated for a free education, or that school material and books should be supplied without charge, or that the Bible lesson should not be given, and caprice, or a groundless, absurd rumour would indispose the ladies to receive the visitor for a day, or a week, or a month, or decline all future intercourse, without any reason alleged, or a false one given ! Now it is far otherwise. Eagerness to learn and a wider acquaintance with Christian ladies and their aims have won for them affection, confidence, and respect. Their visits are often eagerly expected, alike for the instruction and pleasure they afford ; and many men who care little for the education of women encourage these visits, when they perceive that women through them

become brighter and happier, by having their attention
drawn from trifling and sordid affairs to things that
are alike interesting and elevating. Zenana ladies,
therefore, are in a much better position than formerly.
They can secure greater freedom of speech, give such
instruction as they think best, secure attention to
rules, usually make their visits bear a distinctly
'Christian character, and secure payment for their
services—a condition to be steadily kept in view, for
mission work should ever, as a policy, move toward
self-support ; and woman's work, whilst apt to grow
in expenditure, is also apt to fail most in this
direction.

It is unnecessary to refer to the *various forms
zenana instruction takes*, for whilst education may
be given to the young, conversation may be more
interesting to others, and convey to them a great deal
of useful information relative to the great world which
lies outside their own most restricted sphere. It may
with advantage take the form of day schools, Sunday
schools, Bible readings, drawing-room meetings, working parties, social gatherings, gospel addresses, and
is most efficient when it takes these various forms.
Thus, the zenana visitor, be she an Englishwoman
or a native, may give instruction in half a dozen
houses in the course of a day, and have in each
several pupils, the various members of a multitudinous
family, who, though differing greatly in age, may be
of equal grade as learners.

The constantly increasing efficiency of zenana

agency as a means of reaching the higher classes, especially in towns, probably suggested that *Bible women* would be a suitable agency for reaching the far more numerous classes of the poor and low caste. They themselves are usually Christian women of low caste origin, with some knowledge of the Bible and of Christian truth, and an adequate amount of intelligence, zeal, and tact. Their primary duty is to visit the houses or small groups of houses into which towns and even villages are usually divided, to sell portions of Scripture, read or narrate Bible incidents, explain to the women the main features of the gospel, sing hymns, and give instructive and interesting information. To native women, ignorant, inquisitive, solitary, imaginative, despised, and with abundant leisure, such visits are most welcome, and afford fine opportunities for telling of heavenly things.

These feminine colporteurs are usually employed in the cities or villages adjoining; but recently an analogous, but more systematic method of evangelization has been tried in a few instances.

Two or more ladies with native assistants live in a convenient village centre, and do what they can to evangelize all places within their reach, by conversation, teaching, familiar gospel addresses, and living out the Christian life by acts of unselfishness and benevolence. Villages, not towns, are the great feature of Indian social life,[1] and there are literally

---

[1] At the last census, returns were received from 717,549 places, but only 2085 of these ranked as towns, all the remainder being villages,

tens of thousands of villages into which the gospel has never been taken. Such missions are admirably fitted to reach a large class hitherto untouched by any Christian agency. But they require special qualifications. Happily, English women are free to travel all over India without fear of violence, though not of fraud. They may go safely for hundreds of miles by private conveyance without meeting a European. They may live with none but native servants near them, and meet with the utmost courtesy, though it must be added that they will be cheated in every business transaction, and all portable property silently disappear, unless they are watchful and know the ways of the people, but they themselves will be treated with the utmost respect and even politeness! Cheating and overcharging Europeans are in the eyes even of native servants looked on as quite permissible, and they assume an air of wounded innocence if called what they really are, but violence and insult from them are almost unknown.

For women thus occupied, native women as servants and assistants are necessary. So are courage, good health, tact, a knowledge of the language and of native customs, and much zeal and self-denial, otherwise such work becomes expensive and degenerates into routine. But given these, and it becomes angelic.

the urban population being 9·48 per cent., the rural 90·52. In England 53 per cent. of the population reside in 182 towns of 20,000 and upward. In India there are 227 such towns, yet only 4·84 per cent. of the population reside in them.

The lady missionary may gain access where no other European can enter. She is the bearer of a Divine and most gracious message to those who need it sorely. She is welcomed as a woman by women, but invested with strange power and charm, for she is of foreign race, from a land of mysteries and marvels, can read and write, and is free. She can fulfil her beneficent mission by instruction, by conversation, by inquiry, by words of consolation and hope, or by ministering to the diseased and ill.

If she is interested in the strange mysteries of native character and customs, she has the best of all opportunities for such studies, and may have the feminine, innocent pleasure of knowing that probably she was the first European lady who spoke to her dark sisters, and that her visit and her words will be a subject of wonder and conversation for many days. Not only in the village where she lives, but in all others within reasonable distance, she may gain more free access to all the people than any other European, and a sweeter and holier influence. Miss Tucker—A.L.O.E. of Batala—was a fine instance of what may be done in this direction.

Medical Missions have in recent years much increased in number and efficiency. Much was done formerly in an unprofessional way by missionaries, to relieve the sick. Then followed some slight training for zenana and other teachers, and finally the designation of specially trained lady doctors to mission stations, in charge of hospitals, or for itineration through country districts where their services were most needed.

The application of medical and surgical skill as an evangelizing agency must necessarily be restricted, but is of great value. Credible report affirms that Hindu women suffer much from general ill health and some forms of disease, whilst native treatment is pretentious and empirical. A skilled lady doctor is therefore the most welcome of visitors alike to the purdah lady who dreads to leave the seclusion of the zenana, and the low-caste woman whose poverty, timidity, or illness is a formidable obstacle to her going far for the advice she so greatly needs.

The number of lady missionaries sent out who have some surgical training is now considerable, and in India such training is in a few instances given to native women.

But the most important of all such agencies, alike in skilful and various training and extent of operation, is the Countess of Dufferin's Fund. As the expression of British philanthropy, initiated and carried to a splendid issue by the most illustrious lady in India, with the generous aid of native princes of the highest rank, it has been an object-lesson of the highest value in humanity, benevolence, and mindfulness of women, to the whole empire, whilst as a means of relief from all forms of suffering and disease to which women are liable its value cannot be described. Happily, it is placed on a firm and permanent basis, though needing, and worthy of, yet larger funds, so that it will in future years, as now, 'be like a well-watered garden, and like a spring of water whose waters fail not.'

The direct and indirect success of female missionary agency has led to some useful, though subordinate, forms of it, such as homes for native inquirers and converts, and schools and homes of industry.

All converts, but especially women, are in most difficult positions, and so often are missionaries. A text of Scripture, a word spoken, an incident, a report brought into a zenana by a school-boy of what he hears at school, the visit of a Bible woman or zenana lady, may awaken in a woman a yearning wish to know more of God and of Jesus Christ whom He hath sent. But how can she learn more ? She cannot read or write. She cannot go to any Christian for instruction, or invite any one to come to her. To do this would awaken sleepless bigotry and watchfulness to thwart her purpose, if she be a true woman. Or a bad woman, for revenge, or through a family feud, or to escape intolerable ill-treatment, or some mistaken ideas of Christian liberty, may desire to profess the Christian faith, and throw herself on the protection of the mission. Her story may be plausible, but it would be equally unwise to reject her at once or baptize her.

It is advisable to shelter and protect such without compromising either the woman or the missionary. A house is therefore provided for such, where for a few days or weeks their case may be inquired into, their purposes determined, and they be taught the essential truths of the Gospel before baptism.

Then often comes the difficulty of providing for such converts. Their own families usually cast them off utterly. They are, it must be admitted, very helpless and unfitted to fight the battle of life, and for them to be supported by the mission is neither good nor wise. And spheres of employment for such, and indeed, for all women, are exceedingly limited. Hence the importance of training them, if sufficiently gifted, to be teachers ; if not, for some employment taught in industrial schools.

The systematic training of lady missionaries for foreign service now engages much attention, yet not as much as its importance demands. The medical training of a few is complete, and in this direction the Countess of Dufferin's Fund is of the highest value.

For purposes of *educational training*, great progress has been made among native Christian and Eurasian women. Thus should it be. They are there ; they know the language ; they are familiar with the habits of the people ; and as Christianity extends it is inevitable that its propagation and every form of ministry should pass more and more into their hands.

The number of societies and associations now working for women, and their various auxiliary forms of agency, need not be minutely described. In addition to some independent societies, such as the Zenana, Bible, and Medical Mission, and Indian Female Normal School and Instruction Society, founded in

1852, but since considerably extended in its range of operations, most of the leading missionary societies have now associations or auxiliaries specially for Indian women. So it is with the great American societies labouring in India, and to a less degree with the German and other Continental societies. School teaching, zenana visitation and instruction, medical work, village evangelization, are the principal directions in which they act. What is now required is not so much new methods of work, as a wise, economical, earnest prosecution of those in use, and an extension of them, for the agents bear but a most inadequate proportion to the spheres already open. And these spheres must widen and extend.

LADY DUFFERIN'S CHRISTIAN GIRLS' SCHOOL (LAHORE).

CHAPTER XV.

THE deep-rooted and crushing nature of the evils identified with the lot of women throughout India should afford a sufficient motive for exertion on their behalf. For these evils affect not a class, but more or less all women. They press on them from the cradle to the grave ; they affect not only the practical life in all its details of tens of millions, but the lot of all ; and some of the usages affecting their state produce an aggregate amount of suffering it is appalling to imagine. For instance, slavery is more brutalizing than perpetual widowhood with its associated customs, but the aggregate amount of suffering and sorrow arising out of slavery in the British Colonies or the United States did not, I believe, equal that arising out of the latter custom among the Hindus. A lack of information as to the actual facts, or a want of imagination, or an unwillingness to look the facts in the face, lest our selfish quietness should be disturbed, hinders us from realizing the vast amount of physical and mental suffering such a custom has produced, year after year for centuries, on these patient, unoffending millions ; but if in any measure it were realized, it would move us to pity and indignation, as no revelation of wrong and suffering has ever done.

And there are certain features of our enterprise for the good of Hindu women that are most encouraging. Some, as freedom for all forms of beneficent labour, have already been alluded to. It is a remarkable feature of our rule that the Christian evangelist is free to go anywhere, to declare all Christian truth, and to use every form of agency for the overthrow of evil customs. This, it may be said, is but what we should expect from British supremacy, but it should be remembered that nothing like the same freedom of opinion and practice for missionaries and their converts has ever been tolerated in India before, or in any country not Christian and Protestant.

And the latent intolerance, not of Mahomedans only, but of Hindus, is seen in almost every instance in which a Hindu of high caste, or a Mahomedan, has the courage of his convictions, and becomes a Christian.

Our opportunities for free and continuous effort are unique, and should be used with corresponding eagerness. God has set before us a wide and open door, and great is our responsibility if we enter not in.

And there are encouragements to labour of a different kind.

The better instincts of Hindu human nature are on our side. The people are by no means blind to the evils inherent in their own religious and social system. Their great intellectual insight, their strong affections and humane instincts, cause them to respond to our ideas of right, justice, and humanity. Therefore it has been easy for us—far more easy than was anticipated—to suppress infanticide, suttee, and the cruelty and obscenity often associated with religious festivals. And so, when child marriage is condemned, the age of consent raised, widow marriage approved, the higher status of women, with more freedom and courteous treatment, advocated, it finds a ready response in the minds of great numbers.

And opinion in favour of these reforms gathers strength with advancing years. Prudence, indeed, is required as well as wisdom, in the government of a people so suspicious and sensitive; but ours has always had a large share of both, and therefore it is that no Government enactment on social questions has ever provoked formidable opposition or general discontent.

Happily, our teaching on the subjects in question is sustained by our example, in two ways.

1. Family life in official circles was never so pure as it is now.

2. There are now schools with scholars scattered

over India. In a considerable number of these a good English education, based on Christian principles, is given, and in all of them, though no lessons on woman's rights are directly taught, the general drift of instruction and sentiment is in favour of change. The simple fact that Government and missionaries alike encourage the establishment of girls' schools does this. In all these schools it is inevitable that the burning questions relating to the difference between Christian and Hindu customs regarding the treatment of women should be raised, if not in the schools, as an inevitable result of the instruction there given. Next, indeed, to the great questions of religion, these are the most considered; and whilst it must be admitted that few Hindus fully recognize the evils of their own system, and are prepared to adopt anything like the English standard for the status of women, there are hardly any who do not admit the existence of great abuses and evils, and advocate an advance at least in the English direction. Greater freedom for women and a nearer approach to equality with men, re-marriage, the evils of child marriage, the advantages of female education and kindred questions are all topics of general interest, and all public and general opinion on the part of the educated is far in advance of what it was a few years ago.

And example encourages this advance. European family life is rarer in India than is supposed; for, apart from the far too great number of British soldiers, there

are not 50,000 Europeans scattered over the empire.
But among these, and especially where missionaries
are stationed, the freedom, beauty, and pleasantness of
domestic life are usually seen. It is not obtrusive, for
the English are a race given to reserve, but natives
are observant, especially of usages different to their
own, and servants are numerous. It is observed, and
quietly talked of, that an English woman is free to
enter into every part of a house, to leave it, to ride,
or walk, or visit at pleasure ; that she freely receives
guests of both sexes, sits at the same table as her
husband ; speaks and acts with freedom, and as the
equal of men ; reads and writes, seems happy, and is
ever treated with respect and courtesy. That which
to us is a matter of course is to them an object-lesson
of deep significance ; and though inclined usually to
assume that the opinions and usages of other races do
not concern them, except as curious pieces of information, yet the practical nature of all questions relating
to the status and treatment of women became so to
them, since the evils inherent in native society are
obvious to all the educated, and to women especially.
A new and happier world is opened when they
read and hear of Christian principles and English
usages.

It is a stimulus and incentive to all who aid in
female missions that, in spite of manifold difficulties
and intense prejudices, the work has so far advanced,
is now so popular and is in all its details progressive.
There have been, as we have shown, extraordinary

difficulties, and, as we shall show, there are details in its prosecution that wear and worry all zealous and active minds. But the greatest obstacles and the most inveterate have been overcome. Government has declared in favour of female education, and has established and encouraged the formation of thousands of schools. Women are the equals of men in the eyes of the law, and education not only does not injure them or trouble family life, but it elevates the latter, and brings to the former a new source of interest and of happiness.

To us these are matters of course, so obviously just and humane that some may deem it superfluous to name them, but each in native estimation marks a vast change, a great social revolution ; and now, after centuries of systematic and heartless repression, during which no effort for their relief in any one direction was made, and half a century of patient labour, we see the beginning of one of the greatest social changes in public sentiment the world has ever witnessed. Every European who can contrast the India of the first half of the century with the India of to-day must be astonished at the progress made. The people themselves marvel at the change, though they do not fully understand or appreciate its bene-ficence ; and of all the indirect blessings missions have conferred on heathen races—of which the world takes small account—this is the greatest. We see yet but the day of small things, for the men of advanced views and the women taught and free, are a mere fraction of the population ; but advance is now inevitable.

It is a remarkable feature of Puranic or popular Hinduism that any intelligent person who once begins to doubt its character and claims, can never find rest and content in what he formerly accepted. He may apparently remain the same, but intellectually he must be a different person. Hinduism has no foundation in reason or science or history. It cannot possibly satisfy the inquiries and wants of an intelligent seeking soul. This is mainly because it contradicts the plain facts of physical science. In like manner, but for a different reason, the customs affecting the status of women cannot remain as they were. Intense conservatism may lead the old and ignorant to cling to the past, but all who become in any sense educated or observant see the injustice and impolicy of the old usages, and in their timidity may advocate slow or partial reforms. They may plead for the subordination of women to men, and for limitations on their freedom, but that they should be taught to read and write and have more freedom, and be treated with more deference and respect are opinions now held by all who claim to be educated and intelligent. It is indeed astonishing how opinion on all such questions has advanced in half a century, and with accelerated speed and force. This is explained by a feature of the Hindu character, their extreme conservatism and timidity causing them to dread and dislike change.

On all practical questions a long leavening process must precede any open and avowed change. It is very rare for any one to act on his own personal convictions ; each one waits for his neighbour. They hold back from taking the hazardous leap, as a flock of sheep, until one bolder or rasher than the rest rushes forward, and then all follow. It is therefore a remarkable feature of native society that after long delay, and almost sullen, passive resistance, one evil after another has given way, never more to be defended or practised. And on other questions opinion is year by year becoming more general and advanced. It is a signal proof of social progress and of Christian triumph over difficulties that some of us can look back to the time when it was difficult to find spheres for lady missionaries, however zealous and gifted, and now it is difficult to find in sufficient numbers women well qualified for the varied spheres open for them.

Work among the women of India appeals most strongly and tenderly to the love, compassion, and zeal of all Christian women. There is nowhere in all the world so prodigious a number of human beings so enthralled, so suffering, and so helpless. And year by year their prison doors are being opened, and they made more accessible to every form of beneficent endeavour. This should animate our Christian zeal, and all the resources and agencies required for a work so stupendous, varied, and hopeful should be readily supplied. But we should work wisely as well as

SCENE IN BANGALORE HOSPITAL.

zealously; the quality and qualifications even much
more than the number of our missionaries need to be
considered. No woman should enter the missionary
sphere who is not prepared to endure hardness as a
good soldier of Jesus Christ. The timid, the indolent,
the selfish, the unsympathetic, had best refrain from
a service which may give them employment, but in
which they will find little gladness, and gain no great
success; for the Indian climate is most exhausting,
much of the work is monotonous, and not a few
women visited and taught are hopelessly dull, superstitious, indolent, and degraded. But there is another
side which appeals strongly to all of true missionary
spirit. The work is now so varied that Christian
women may find in it an ample sphere, if the requisite
skill, tact, judgment, sympathy, and zeal are possessed.
For some, such work has intense fascination, and for
others a divine joy. Surely it is such service as angels
would delight in. Even for the study of human
nature and the manners and customs of a remarkable
people, some forms of women's work offer unusual
opportunities.

And the low estate of women in all the aspects of
life offers a great stimulus to exertion on their behalf,
because whatever is done is greatly needed to be done,
and tells distinctly toward their relief and elevation.
English women, though ignorant and unhappy, yet
know so much, and have so many sources of comfort
that, except in extreme cases, it is difficult, and only
by a slow process, that their knowledge can be

increased or their character elevated. On the other hand, every lesson taught to Hindu women is a distinct advance in their education ; every visit is an event looked forward to with interest, remembered with pleasure ; and every lesson taught conveys new and important information affecting this life, or may be a revelation of hope and salvation for the life to come.

There is a feature of this Indian work most interesting and encouraging that the writer has never seen noticed. It is this. Not only does the position of Indian women give them an attractive conception of all the qualities in Christ and Christianity which make for their relief and elevation, but Hindu human nature is profoundly religious and responsive to the genius and spirit of the Gospel.

Human nature is everywhere depraved, but, however varied, none are beyond the divine, renovating power of Christian truth when applied to the heart and life by the Spirit of God. It is the ' power of God unto salvation ' for all. But as there are degrees of intellectual power, of moral integrity, of refinement and devoutness among persons, so are there among races. No race is more naturally devout and refined, a refinement that is sympathetic with the characteristics of patience, gentleness, and submission, than the Hindus. No people pray more, worship more, talk more of religion. They have a sympathy with religion in its general features, and a susceptibility for devotion that is very impressive.

I cannot but think that in India there is more of the good ground, and less of the stony, into which the good seed of the kingdom may fall than in other lands—in our own, for instance—and that when superstition is weakened, and the Gospel more generally preached and better understood, it will be more generally welcomed than elsewhere, take more complete possession of the whole personality, and develop types of saintliness which for beauty, heavenliness, and completeness, especially among women, now we seldom see. For has not the word saintly and the quality it indicates become strangely infrequent with us?

There is even a higher aspect of this work. It is most Christ-like. It is not presumptuous to assume that, if the Saviour were now to minister to mankind, He would turn most pityingly to the women of India as the class most in need of His compassion and help, and—I venture to say—most responsive to His mission. The poor, the abject, the ignorant, the neglected, the sorrowful, were those He most pitied and helped when He walked in Galilee. And women had the truest perception of the grace and beauty of His nature, and turned most responsively toward Him. They most felt their need of such a Friend and Deliverer; He could do most for them, therefore they loved the most. He is the same yesterday, to-day, and for ever, and therefore now His love and pity go out unceasingly toward the multitudinous women of the East, so

much in need of His aid. For is not His divine
mission especially adapted to such? He says so.
'The Spirit of the Lord God is upon Me, because
the Lord hath anointed Me to preach good tidings
unto the meek ; He hath sent Me to bind up the
brokenhearted, to proclaim liberty to the captives,
and the opening of the prison to them that are bound ;
to proclaim the acceptable year of the Lord, and
the day of vengeance of our God ; to comfort all that
mourn ; to appoint unto them that mourn in Zion, to
give unto them beauty for ashes, the oil of joy for
mourning, the garment of praise for the spirit of
heaviness; that they might be called trees of
righteousness, the planting of the Lord, that He might
be glorified.'

It is not surprising that Hindu women listen with
ever rapt attention to the story of His life and
death ; love most the hymns which describe what
He said and did ; and so often say, 'Your Shastras
must have been written by women; they speak so
tenderly of us.'

There is a misconception relating to the extent and
need of women's work it is important to correct.
When ladies hear that there are at least 760 foreign
and European female missionaries with 3500 native
Christian women engaged in school, zenana, town
and village evangelization, and that Hindu opinion
on all social subjects is changing greatly for the
better, they are apt to assume that sufficient is
being done, and that progress is far greater than it

really is; they forget the law of proportions; they observe what has been done; they overlook what remains to be done, and they can have no conception of the profound and inveterate torpor pervading the East. Usages and customs, even the face of nature and the appearances of human life, hardly change with the centuries. It is a vast lotus land, where things seem to live in dreamy lethargy from which they have no desire to awaken. Tennyson's *Lotus Eaters* express the sentiment of the entire East.

> 'Let us alone. Time driveth onward fast,
> And in a little while our lips are dumb.
> Let us alone. What is it that will last?
> All things are taken from us, and become
> Portions and parcels of the dreadful past.
> Let us alone. What pleasure can we have
> To war with evil? Is there any peace
> In ever climbing up the climbing wave?
> All things have rest and ripen toward the grave
> In silence; ripen, fall, and cease :
> Give us long rest or death, dark death or dreamful ease.'

The great mass of the people desire no change, wish to be let alone, dislike our restless energy, and look on us as a painful, mysterious dispensation of Providence that they must endure, but cannot comprehend.

But whilst we rejoice in what has been accomplished, and see in it the presage of coming triumphs, it is important to realize that far more remains to be done than has yet been accomplished. Think of the vast

extent of country that needs to be reached—an area
equal to at least twelve Englands ; of the dead weight
of torpor, ignorance, prejudice, suspicion, we have
to contend with ; the tens of millions of women
who need to be reached, educated, comforted, and
elevated. All Protestant societies unite in sending
but one foreign and Eurasian lady missionary to
about each 190,000 of these. Probably not one
zenana in a hundred has ever been entered by a
missionary lady, or half the 715,500 villages of the
empire been visited by any Christian woman, or half
the entire population had the Gospel message even
once presented to them. 'There is much land yet to
be possessed.' 'The harvest truly is plenteous, but
the labourers are few ; pray ye therefore the Lord
of the harvest, that He send forth labourers into His
harvest.'

> 'Our sword has swept o'er India, there remains
> A nobler conquest far—
> The mind's ethereal war,
> That but subdues to civilize its plains.
>
> Let us pay back the past the debt we owe :
> Let us around dispense
> Light, hope, intelligence,
> Till blessings track our steps where'er we go.
>
> O England ! thine be the deliverer's meed ;
> Be thy great empire known
> By hearts made all thine own,
> By thy free laws and thy immortal creed.'

INDEX

—◦◦—

THE END.